RULER OF PERFECTION
T ONYX

Something new
Something mysterious
Something delicious
Enjoy...

PROLOGUE

Negril, Jamaica

"Alright, alright I'll be there. Are you sure about this Rashid? Right …yes, yes, I know. Alright. My flight leaves in three hours. Yeah…yeah see you in the morning."

Kamili Tamu Okonkwo set her slim cellular in the back pocket of the skirt she wore. Closing her eyes resignedly, she appeared to meditate. She indulged in the soothing pastime but a moment before focusing once more on the raw beauty of the setting sun. The view was glorious, but her time to enjoy it had reached its end.

Unfortunately, her nipples were still hard. The sensation of the buds brushing the front of the black silk wrap blouse was a mix of delight and frustration. Kam cursed herself for not wearing a bra with the alluring piece, but then she'd never been shy about flaunting her assets. That is, until she'd started her current architectural endeavor.

Even still, Kam had so grossly underestimated how attentive her host would be that evening. The two year project was at last complete and her firm was on hand to celebrate the meeting. Chisulo Nkosi's latest addition to his museum empire had received worldwide attention. Nkosi possessed so many priceless artifacts; he was as captivating as they were. Of course, it wasn't simply Chisulo's artifacts that made him so entrancing. The man's vicious intensity had the power to make a woman cream her panties just by standing next to him.

Kam vowed that she was different. She wasn't of course, but she'd done a fine job of pretending. She'd managed to interact with him only in the presence of others. In short, she made a point to never be alone with him.

Though on edge about attending the soiree, Kam figured Chisulo would be so busy tending his mob of admirers, he'd have no time to look her way. She was wrong. He was standing right behind her-hence the throbbing boobs and rigid nipples. He was sure to notice her…reaction the moment she turned to face him.

"Shouldn't you be off somewhere in bed with someone?" Kam inquired in a sweet voice laced with steel.

Chisulo Nkosi smiled, his dimples sparked deep beneath the silky onyx whiskers. Those whiskers covered his jaw, combining with the mustache above his heavenly mouth. The affect gave the rich blackberry tone of his skin an even more alluring appearance.

"I'm working on it," Chisulo told Kam. He relaxed his 6 foot plus frame against one of the towering marble columns that shielded the patio from the interior of the house.

Kam rested her hands flat along the stone ledge lining the patio. Her panties were soaking wet now. His canyon deep voice was as powerful an aphrodisiac as the rest of his body. She stiffened when a massive hand appeared on either side of her along the ledge. He moved closer, dipping his head so that his hair just brushed her skin.

"Cold?" he asked.

Clearly, he'd spotted her nipples outlined against the blouse.

Kam didn't try to hide the smile tugging at her mouth. "A little," she admitted seconds before a moan escaped her lips. His hands abandoned the ledge to cover her silk clad bosom. "What the hell are you doing?" she demanded in little more than a whisper.

Chisulo shrugged, commanding himself not to make her turn and face him. "I'm collecting on our bet," he explained instead.

Kam frowned in confusion, in spite of the sensation swirling throughout her body. His thumb and forefinger squeezed and stroked the hardening nipple of one breast, while his other hand weighed its twin. "What bet?" she practically purred, tugging her lower lip between her teeth when his hand plundered inside her blouse.

"Tsk, tsk. Don't tell me you forgot?" he teased, soothing one bare bud of the mound with the pad of his thumb.

What are you doing? Kam silently reprimanded herself, but God what *he* was doing felt so…mmm. She leaned into his touch and indulged in a deep breath which increased the delicious friction of her breasts crushing his wide palms. She felt him close what little distance remained between them and her head leaned back just slightly. It was the almost frightening intensity of a thoroughly stiffened cock that wrenched her from a mesmerized state of mind. Clearing her throat, she maneuvered out of his loose embrace.

"What bet?" she asked again. Her back was still facing him when he offered his reply.

"The bet that involves me having you in my bed if you lost. You lost."

Kam turned at last. Her lovely slanting brown stare narrowed more the longer she studied him. *Dammit fool, pay attention to his words-not his face!* She chastised herself again, for all the good it did. *Studying* Chisulo Nkosi was a difficult thing for any woman to resist. His skin was flawless and dark as obsidian. It stretched taut over a broad muscular frame. His hair was a mass of onyx waves; silky and almost shoulder length. Striking midnight eyes were deep set beneath heavy sleek brows.

"What bet?" Kam forced the words, while closing her eyes on the image of his incredible mouth feasting on her throbbing clit.

Chisulo leaned against the ledge. "The bet we made soon after you came to work for me," he shared and folded his arms across the front of the navy blue linen shirt he wore. "After your accusation?" he said, attempting to spark her memory. He shook his head, grinning as he uttered the 'tsking' sound once more at the sight of her continued bewilderment. "Kami, Kami...so sharp and sexy and yet so forgetful."

Kam bristled as she often did when he shortened her name that way. How many times had she imagined him whispering *Kami* in her ear as he thrust what felt like a magnificently proportioned dick inside her?

Chisulo bowed his head and focused on his stylish loafers one crossed over the other. "You accused me of being a man who couldn't resist making a play for a woman even if she was a colleague or in my employ," he explained before fixing her with his pitch gaze. "In short, you called me a sexist pig and said you'd probably not finish the project for me chasing you around my desk-more or less."

Kam laughed at the absurd statement, but sobered quickly when he didn't share her merriment. "And was I right about you?" she asked.

Chisulo tilted his head, his brows rising skeptically. "Clearly not. I didn't come on to you once the entire time you were working on the museum."

Kam didn't appear impressed. "You must be very proud of yourself?"

"Not easy to be proud when your dick is hard, Kami."

Kam placed a hand on her hip and gaze a flip shrug. "I wouldn't think that's a thing you'd have problems finding someone to handle."

"Generally, it's not."

Kam blinked a hint of recollection beginning to surface remnants of the conversation to which he was referring. "What exactly did we wager?" she breathed, her hand growing weak where it rested on her hip.

Chisulo's smile was arrogance personified. "I think you recall."

"Refresh my memory."

"If I lost, I'd double your already sizable fee to finish the project."

Kam drew closer to the patio ledge. "And if *I* lost?"

Chisulo responded in what sounded every bit like a growl. "I get you. All day-all night. Any time, any place, any *way*."

Kam felt her breath growing increasingly short. "For how long?" she managed to question.

"A week," he told her, smiling when she blinked and rested against the ledge. "I think you were pretty confident I would lose."

Kam's frown reasserted itself, marring her exquisite dark chocolate face. "You didn't take what I said seriously, though?"

Chisulo stroked his jaw, his eyes raking her body when she stood straight. "Kami, sex is something I take very seriously. The freedom to fuck you any way I please for seven days and nights is an opportunity I'd never let pass me by."

Kam shook her head. "You're insane," she accused, her metallic sandalwood wrap heels clicking against the stone patio as she backed away from him slowly.

Chisulo was calm and thoroughly amused. "Kami," he purred.

"*Chisel*," she countered in a hiss, using her own shortening of his name. As their working relationship had traveled into a more familiar realm, she'd adapted the name simply to annoy him. He seemed to adore it.

"Kami please don't act like this is a shock," Chisulo urged. He'd cornered her in the angle where the ledge and a brick wall side of the villa met. "Don't pretend that you don't want it. Especially when I can look at you and tell that you do."

Kam followed the direction of his stare and realized that her nipples had betrayed her. Again, they were hard as tiny pebbles and straining against her blouse. Chisulo rested one hand atop the ledge and let the back of the other brush the rigid nubs. Kam wanted to moan even as she moved to strike him. He caught her wrist in his vice grip before she could complete the act.

Turning the tables, Chisulo held Kam's arm at the small of her back and gave her a tiny jerk. Kam was so angry her lashes practically fluttered close. She was also aroused-so very sweetly aroused. For the second time that night, he imprisoned one of her tits in his hand. His head was bowed while he focused on fondling her. The instant Kam trembled and lost her footing, Chisulo's grip tightened. He raised his head and kissed her, driving his tongue hard and deep inside her mouth.

Kam allowed her moans to escape as she writhed against the powerful male who commanded her every move. In his arms, she still beat a clenched fist against the unyielding width of his chest. Her tongue however, thrust and rotated around his in an almost desperate manner. She suckled the thrusting organ hard and slow as if she were determined to taste every inch. Chisulo uttered the growling sound once more and released her arm to open her blouse.

"Jesus," he whispered, burying his dark, gorgeous face in her heaving cleavage to fill his nostrils with her scent.

Kam cried out into the floral scented Jamaican air while he alternated sucking and grazing his teeth across her milk chocolate breasts. His lips and tongue tugged at her nipples that were pouted and erect before his mouth. Kam buried her fingers in the lush blackness of his beautiful hair and forced him closer. She was grinding against the heart stopping stiffness of his cock, the spiky heels of her sandals moving over his navy trousers as they ascended his pant leg. Her hands moved to cup and squeeze his perfect ass, tugging him against her. She craved the feel of his dick powerfully erect below his waist. She wanted it inside her-filling her-coming inside her again and again…

As though he were breaking out of a spell, Chisulo stopped. His charcoal stare was hooded and intense as it fixed on her lovely face. "I think you've got a plane to catch," he said.

Kam shook violently while trying to tamp down the fire he'd ignited and refused to extinguish. "Shit," she hissed, realizing that she was still grinding herself against his remarkable shaft when he spoke.

Chisulo grinned and pressed a kiss to the corner of her mouth. "Sorry love, but tonight's bad for me anyway. I *am* hosting a party, you know?"

"Son of a bitch," Kam raged, uncurling her fingers from the lapels of his shirt. "You know I won't go through with this foolishness."

Chisulo's grin was purely sinful. "Oh I think you will," he countered softly, forcing her back against the ledge again. Holding her gaze captive with his own, his hand ventured past one of the slits in her skirt.

Kam leaned back her head and bit her lip. He caressed her bare thighs and the lace fringe of her black panties. His index and middle fingers invaded her pussy and were soon covered in heavy cream. Kam braced her hands on the ledge and rode the limbs that pleasured her more than any man's dick ever had. Seconds into the masterful finger fuck, she was in the grips of a strong orgasm. The lips of her sex clenched and released his fingers, milking them as they would his shaft if given the chance.

Chisulo drove his tongue into her ear and; within minutes, brought Kam to a second devastating orgasm. "Be ready when I call," he whispered, when her forehead fell against his shoulder and she tried to catch her breath.

"When?" Kam heard herself and cursed the sound of desperation in her voice.

Chisulo grinned and cupped her chin. "Patience love," he spoke against her mouth and left her with a quick kiss before he was gone.

ONE

Batoka Gorge, Zimbabwe
One Year Later...

"He's alright. He's alright-just taking a few extra minutes...*hours*. Stop it!" Kam ordered herself. But she was desperate for any evidence to support the fact that her brother would return any moment. *Forget it*, she snapped in silence. Rashid should have returned the night before. Dawn was two hours ago and still there was no sign of him.

"To hell with this," she spat, leaving her post along the window sill overlooking the western portion of the property. Kam knew she'd go crazy if she waited any longer. She cast a resigned glance toward the powerful cross bow leaning against one of the deep leather armchairs in the den. Rolling her eyes, she grabbed the weapon and headed for the back door.

Kam made her way to the path she'd seen Rashid take the night before. He left at dusk as he'd done every evening over the last twelve months. Kam's expression grew tight as her thoughts drifted. She and her brother had been alone in this strange situation for the better part of three years. Kam swore to Rashid that he could depend on her. She swore never to run in fear because of the frightful phenomena that had taken root in him.

Before the last few years commenced, shape shifters were only figments of fantasy. They were characters in tales of dragons and witches. They certainly were not living things that roamed the real world.

Rashid Okonkwo, however had completely disproved that theory. Such a figment was exactly who-or what he had become.

"And he's out here," Kam whispered, tugging at the straps that secured the bow on her shoulder. "God please let him be safe," she prayed, rubbing suddenly sweaty palms across the front of the tan suede jacket that molded to her torso. Suddenly, she summoned the courage to quicken her pace.

She'd never questioned Rashid's jaunts, never asked if other tigers roamed with him. She decided a discussion of that life was the very last thing her brother would want to discuss with his baby sister. She simplified her job to cleansing his wounds, preparing meals and trying to provide him with some semblance to a normal *human* existence.

The thought stopped Kam in her tracks. She'd turned her back on a successful architectural firm which held her name emblazoned on its doors. She left the world she knew to follow her brother into danger-into death. *God, please let me find him*, Kam begged, slowing her steps as the atmosphere grew darker and thicker with brush.

A flash of white brought more caution to her face and slowly she pulled the bow from her back. She stood motionless in the clearing, taking vague notice that the sky was almost black as night-a heavy fog settled.

The flash of white whisked by once more and her heart lifted. Rashid. She recognized his white coat striped with black. Her eyes narrowed as her first thought was that he was resting. Instead, he was hunched-about to attack. But attack what? One cue, her brother's opponent came into view: a lion, as huge and as black as the dark surrounding him. Against Rashid the animal was massive almost gargantuan. Kam felt a scream struggling in her throat for release. She kept silent, using every ounce of courage she possessed. The horrific looking feline could very well render her unconscious-or worse-with one swat of a mighty paw.

Surely Rashid can defend himself, Kam reasoned. After all, he'd gone out night after night and returned alive-at *least* alive. She thought, recalling the horrid wounds that marred his body on more than one occasion.

Kam focused in on the black lion again. This beast-this monster… perhaps this was Rashid's first battle against it. Kam feared it threatened to be a meeting her brother may never return from. Without further hesitation, she readied her bow, aimed and fired. Though skilled and possessing expert marksmanship, Kam missed her target. No doubt her nerves were getting the better of her. Still, she got the attention of the two battling cats. The black lion focused in on her at once as if he'd known she was there all along.

Kam rose to her full height, but could make no further movement. She was paralyzed yes, but fear was not the cause. The feline's presence held her captive. His silky black mane was wild and full, the eyes were deep-set and flashed with onyx fire. Kam's hand weakened around her bow.

Rashid capitalized on his opponent's distraction and struck. Kam dropped her bow when she heard her brother roar and charge for the bigger cat. The lion barely acknowledged the unarguably lethal attack.

Kam's eyes grew wide with surprise. For an instant, she could've sworn the black lion wasn't of a mind to scuffle with her brother. Rashid however seemed to be of a mind for a battle regardless of the outcome.

The lion shook off Rashid and accompanied the 'shake' with a vicious roar laced with a rumbling growl. Unexpectedly, it raced off toward the heavier brush. Rashid gave chase.

"No," Kam breathed and a wave of weakness attacked her legs. She lost sight of the felines but remained in pursuit as she disappeared into the foreboding wood.

"You'd have an easier time accomplishing this by rushing out before a speeding bus." Chisulo muttered, now hunched on hands and knees as he attempted to catch his breath.

Lying nude several feet away, Rashid winced but managed a smile. "What can I say?...I like doing things the hard way. Besides...it has to be done."

"Doesn't *have* to be done," Chisulo remained hunched savoring the fresh air filling his system. "Are you forgetting the serum, you idiot? Hell this could all be over in a matter of-"

"Dammit Chisulo listen to yourself. You sound like some daydreaming girl."

"Daydreams have their uses."

"Hell man," Rashid winced again, "they don't even know how to make it work."

Chisulo raked a hand through his hair. "If I do this, your sister will hate me forever."

Rashid smiled. "You love her."

"I want her in my bed."

"You love her and you know the rules."

"Fuck 'em."

"Easier said...you know if you ever expect to have Kam-*any* of her-you have to kill the man who holds the most of her heart." He tapped a finger to his chest. "That'd be me."

"There's another way. We'll find it." Chisulo shook his head while staring out into the blinding thickness of brush. "I've never been one to abide by rules and I won't start now." He turned his head slightly. "I'm sorry man...I can't help you this way. I can't kill you."

"You already have."

Then, Chisulo took note of the strain in Rashid's voice. How long had it been there? He turned and scrambled over to the tree where Rashid rested against the massive trunk.

"God," Chisulo moaned; realizing that Rashid had landed on a heavy branch during the chase and scuffle that transpired once Rashid caught up to him again.

"Thank you." Rashid whispered.

Clenching his jaw, Chisulo looked for the wound and saw that the man was impaled on a branch protruding from the trunk. Bowing his head, Chisulo closed Rashid's eyes and said a prayer for the dead man. His intention was to bury him, but footfalls in the distance alerted him to Kam's approach. Casting one last look upon Rashid's torn body, Chisulo left the clearing.

"No!" Kam cried, her hands clutching the wavy black braid that snaked around her head. "Rashid," her brother's name was barely a whisper when she found him against the massive tree trunk.

Rashid now lay as a man at the base of the tree. Kam broke into a run, dropping beside her brother. Gently, she pulled him from the gored branch and held him against her chest. "Rashid? Rashid? It's Kam, Rashid?" she called, knowing he was dead. Cradling his dark, bare body, she rocked him. The water that filled her eyes, eventually dried. Her sorrow was replaced by hate. Kissing Rashid's forehead, Kam placed him down on the leaves, twigs and bark which littered the ground.

"I'll get him. I promise I will," she vowed, promising death to the beast who had slain her brother.

***

Kam wore a set look as she packed her saddle the next morning. She sat with Rashid's body into the late afternoon and buried him at dusk. For a brief time, the harsh mask of hate left her face to allow regret to take its place. So many times she'd planned to threaten Rashid with leaving if he didn't stop the jaunts that kept him away from her each night. She *had* planned...and now she'd have to live with the results of not following through. While she couldn't bring back her brother, she could stay true to her vow. The black lion would pay. Focusing on making that happen was the one thing that had kept her from lying down and dying right along side Rashid.

Satisfied, that she'd packed an ample supply of weapons and ammunition, Kam patted the rump of her black stallion Coal. Bowing her head, she prayed for courage. Of course, the lone daughter in a family of men had never lacked courage. Kam was beauty and strength incarnate. Her skin was a cool, rich shade of chocolate. She wore her thick wavy hair in heavy twisted ropes that brushed the small of her back when left unbound. Tall and athletic; yet voluptuous and undeniably feminine, she could evoke reverence and arousal in any man.

Kam took a deep breath and closed her eyes again. "Come on, dammit!" she ordered herself to get a move on. She secured the house never knowing when a group of wanderers might happen upon the secluded dwelling.

Kam could never convince Rashid to tell her how he'd snagged the remote villa and surrounding property along the gorge at the base of the heavenly Victoria Falls. It was like living amidst a dream. The area was sought after by tourists and natives alike. In the year they'd lived there, Kam had yet to trek to the top of the mythical site.

One day, she promised herself. Now, there were more pressing issues to occupy her time. Unless she emerged the victor from this bout with the black lion, she'd not live to see the Falls or anything else. On cue, it seemed, a quick flash of movement caught her eyes. Kam stiffened, hoping to catch another glimpse and then-there it was. The wild black mane and the engrossing stare of the onyx cat. Kam didn't blink as she mounted Coal. Urging the great horse to a gallop, she began her pursuit.

The lion remained in her sights. It had to know she was there, didn't it. *Well fuck him if he was letting his guard down*, Kam told herself. She took hold of her bow and arrow, leaving Coal to direct them without supervision. Wasting no more time, she aimed, fired and missed.

"Shit," she readied the bow again.

Again, she missed. The same held true for the next few tries. Kam checked her weapon-it was as if this beast carried some sort of force field around it-protecting it from harm. She was in the midst of studying the arrow, when the thunderous roar filled the air. A flurry of movement followed. Kam tumbled off Coal's back when he reared up and lost his footing. The bow landed on the ground, arrows scattering next just seconds before Kam hit. Her head struck a decaying log and everything went black.

TWO

It wasn't necessary to strip her of every stitch of clothing she wore. Hell, it was only a bump on her head. Still…she could've sustained other injuries, right. *Sounds good Chisulo, think she'll buy it?* He didn't care then. He'd spent the last two hours watching her in his bed as she slept off the injury.

God, she was a beauty, he thought-all chocolate and naked atop the furs covering his bed. A grimace sharpened his magnificent features and he resituated his thoroughly stiff cock where it strained painfully against his button fly. Resting his head against the back of the armchair he occupied, he continued to study her. Now she was his for the taking and he damn well intended to take her and take her and take her…

From the day she'd come to work for him, he'd thought of little else. Making Kamili Okonkwo come until she was too exhausted to even cry out; as he continued to drive himself inside her, had tortured his mind and kept him awake nights on end.

Chisulo heard soft moans rousing from the bed and he sat a bit straighter in the enormous gray chair. His dick lengthened a few more inches beneath his jeans. The organ stiffened even more painfully the longer he watched her writhe on the furs. A moan almost sounded from the back of his own throat as he observed Kam. Her hair had unraveled from the rope-like twists and now covered her face which was buried deep into the coverlets. Chisulo watched, propping his chin against his fist while Kam pushed herself up on the bed. She was still for a moment and then pulled one hand through her hair. Slowly, she turned on the bed and looked across her shoulder. Her eyes narrowed. It was barely eleven a.m., yet the spacious room possessed many dim areas.

Chisulo knew she was trying to determine if there was another body in the room. Perhaps there were simply dark shadows playing tricks on her eyes. Chisulo decided to ease her mind-or at least her curiosity.

He heard her gasp and he smiled; watching her gaze widen and ascend when he stood from the chair and move into the light of the room. She was facing him from the bed-deliciously tousled and expectant. Chisulo clenched his fist at the sight of those perfect tits quickly falling and rising as her breath raced. He'd be settled between those lush thighs, his face full of the chocolate mounds by nightfall, he swore. Not a chance of that happening, if the look on her face were any sign, he decided, stifling the chuckle that threatened to break free.

He neared the bed, watching as her wariness turned to recognition, surprise and then exasperation.

"You," she breathed.

"Me," Chisulo confirmed, his pitch black stare sparkling with devilment.

Kam heard the voice-the orgasm inducing voice, but closed her eyes anyway in case she was hallucinating. She wasn't. He was there alright. Chisulo Nkosi was standing within her reach. Her cocoa stare roamed his incredible face then traveled to the broad chest partially visible beneath his open shirt. The brick expanse of his torso heaved slowly, subtly powerful was the movement. Kam appraised the carved abs and on past the waistband of the loose-fitting dark denims he wore. He was always prepared, she'd give him that-eyeing the bulge of his cock-stiff and ready.

Dammit, Kam, she hissed silently and looked away from him. Focus on the real issue, she commanded herself. "What the hell are you doing here? Where am I?" she demanded to know.

The devilishness in his steady midnight stare grew more sinful. Chisulo moved closer, until the vicinity below his waist was positioned in direct line with Kam's suddenly dry mouth. Her lips actually parted in subconscious anticipation of obliging his unspoken request.

His actions, however, were purely hospitable. Kam didn't know if she were relieved or angry when he simply reached behind her for the lovely mosaic print robe that rested across the headboard. She blinked when he passed her the garment. It was then that she noticed she was completely naked.

"How-?" she gasped, too shocked and embarrassed to finish the question. Quickly, she snatched the robe from his hand. Her expression cleared when Chisulo stepped back, but made no move to give her privacy.

"I don't think we have many secrets left between us, do you Kami?" he purred, delighted when she sneered and practically shoved her arms into the garment's sleeves.

"On the contrary, *Chisel*. We still have quite a few that count."

"Not for long," he guaranteed.

The robe in place, Kam folded her arms beneath her breasts. "For the second time, where am I? And what the hell are you doing here?"

Chisulo made himself comfortable. Lounging back at the foot of the bed, he braced his weight on one elbow and studied her.

Without hesitation, Kam moved back on the bed. She wasn't quite ready to leave the luxurious furs, but she certainly didn't trust herself too close to the dark sexy god who shared them with her.

"You're in my home," he said.

Kam blinked. "*Your* home? But how-"

"Right next to the Falls and not part of the park. Travelers never... *happen* upon my property," he explained.

Kam was silent for a while. So he lived near the Falls. A deep cold riddled her bones to know he'd been so close. She focused in on him again, shaking away the haze that clouded her mind. "Travelers never happen upon your property, you say? Does that go for the female travelers as well?"

Chisulo closed his eyes and smiled. "You wound me, Kami."

"Why am I here?" she asked. Longingly, she stared past the lone window across the room. Her mind was stuck on getting out of the dark bedchamber and viewing Victoria Falls up close.

"You took a tumble on your horse. Got a nasty bump on the head for your trouble," he explained, the words spilling from his sensual mouth as slowly as the manner in which his eyes trailed her bare legs. "My men brought you here."

"Hmph. How hospitable of them and how convenient for you," Kam whispered, her stare screaming suspicion. She shrugged. "I thank you anyway and now if you'd tell me where my clothes are, I'll be on my way."

Chisulo smiled and continued to relax on the bed. He watched her bolt to the heavy double doors.

"Let me out," she ordered, upon discovering the doors wouldn't open.

"It's for your own protection that they're locked," Chisulo explained.

Kam grimaced. "Bullshit," she countered, flashing him a scathing glare when she looked across her shoulder.

Chisulo was still maddeningly calm, resting across the bed with his hands folded across his chest. "Love, while my men are hospitable they aren't so gentlemanly as to let a delicious piece of-a beauty such as you," he rephrased when her eyes narrowed, "walk by them practically naked and not help themselves."

Kam turned, resting her back against the door. "And I suppose you condone such behavior?"

"They know they're dead men if they touch you," Chisulo answered without a second's hesitation. Then, he shrugged and the playfulness returned to his handsome face. "Still...a man may be willing to risk his life for a taste of the sweetness he's sure to find...within."

"Bastard," Kam hissed, though she couldn't fight the shiver his leering stare struck inside her.

Again, Chisulo shrugged. "Feel free to test me. They'll take turns with you, until they make you fuck them two, three at a time."

Kam lost the tether hold on her temper and let loose a frustrated cry. She rushed to the bed. Her fists were clenched and fell upon Chisulo. She beat at his chest with hard, relentless blows. Faintly, she told herself the pounding was providing no pain to the recipient. She didn't care. Her loss, her anger, everything that happened tore her restraint to sheds. She simply wanted to vent her frustrations and the infuriating man beneath her was the perfect victim.

Chisulo was aware of this and allowed Kam to spend her strength. He absorbed her blows, watching as her hair flew wild about them. The satiny dark robe tumbled past her shoulders amidst the frenzy of her movements. Eventually, the punches she laid on his chest and abdomen lost their power.

Chisulo turned the tables then, trapping her beneath his virile form. The robe became twisted about her thighs, leaving the rest of her body bare and trembling.

Kam watched as he took stock of her appearance. His sinful, dark gaze was thorough in its appraisal. "Could I please have my clothes?" she inquired in the most polite manner she could muster.

"Ruined," Chisulo said, keeping his leg thrown across her thighs. "We had to toss them."

"Convenient-again," Kam accused softly, swallowing when he looked into her eyes.

"I could send my men for your things, but it may be a while before they return."

"Don't trouble yourself. The robe'll do until I can get my horse and get the hell out of here," Kam decided, just barely straining against him.

Again, Chisulo fixed his lovely captive with a mockingly regretful stare. "I'm afraid your horse sustained injury as well."

Kam blinked. "Where is he?"

"Here-we're caring for him."

"You-you are?"

"Hell yes," Chisulo chuckled. "What'd you think? That we'd leave him to his death down there?"

Kam shrugged.

Chisulo didn't appear offended. "Even an animal deserves the right to have his wounds tended, don't you agree?"

Kam's lashes fluttered against the pressure of tears. "Yes," she breathed, her expression harboring a look close to grief. "Yes, I do," she repeated.

Chisulo didn't press her to elaborate. He didn't need to. Instead he focused on her-literally. Kam blinked becoming more aware of their position atop the furs.

"You can get off now," she told him.

Chisulo's grin had a wolfish intensity when he whipped away the robe that entwined her thighs. "May I?" he asked.

Kam resisted the urge to bristle, knowing it would only thrust her bosom deeper into his chest. "Get off me," she rephrased, her lips tightening to a thin line when he didn't move. "So I guess you're even less of a gentleman than your men?" she whispered.

Chisulo settled himself between her thighs; nudging her pussy with the bulge of his dick. "Far less," he admitted, adoring the way her lips parted as her lashes fluttered in response. Slowly, he began to thrust against her. Silently, he cursed the jeans that kept him from really touching her.

Kam bit her bottom lip while grinding her moist clit against him. "Chisel...shit..." she hissed, hating what he was making her feel-hating the pleasure only *he* could give her. "Let me go," she asked, but entwined her legs about his as she spoke.

"Let me stay," he urged.

Kam shuddered when his voice rumbled through her trembling frame. The crisp whiskers of his beard rubbed her bare skin, producing the most delicious friction. His denims cut into her flesh and she moaned at the pleasure of the sensation.

"Let me stay," he urged once more, his voice resembling a low growl that sent a trickle of come oozing across her swollen labia.

"I can't," she moaned. Her hands were trapped between their bodies when he covered her and began to suck her earlobe.

"You still owe me, you know?" he coolly reminded her before driving his tongue inside her ear. His fingers brushed the spot between her buttocks. "I could press the issue," he warned, plunging the tip of his thumb just inside the sensitive haven.

Kam gasped, pressing her head into the bed and arching up for more of the caress. Then, she forced her eyes to his. "What issue?" she asked.

Chisulo's massive hands cupped her tits. His nose began to encircle the rigid dark tips. "We still have a bet to settle," he reminded her.

In spite of his weight covering her, Kam managed to laugh. "Are you serious?" she gasped again.

"Deadly," he promised and filled his mouth with her cleavage.

"Mmm," the sound came out all shaky and helpless. Kam buried her fingers in her hair and pushed more of one throbbing breast into his mouth. "That was a year ago," she moaned.

"And I hate like hell I only get you for a week," he muttered, in the midst of his ravenous feasting on one bouncing mound of flesh. "I need at least a life time," he whispered, his perfect teeth biting her nipple.

"Wait," she pleaded, intending to tug on his hair and pull him away. Instead, she lost herself in the rich thickness of the dark crop. She pulled him closer and opened her eyes to watch him nibble the hard nub and then flick it with his tongue. "Please," she begged, needing him to suck the bud deeper inside his mouth. "Please," she gasped again, arching her back so that it only brushed his lips. She sobbed when he ignored her request.

Chisulo abandoned her nipples. He preferred to nudge the perfect pouting endowments with his nose before gliding his tongue across the satiny skin underneath. His mouth was everywhere, lavishing her ribcage and tummy with a shower of kisses. He tongued her belly button, pressing her hips to the bed when she arched reflexively. His kisses turned ragged, wetter, leaving a trail of moisture down her abdomen. The trail journeyed toward her womanhood. Chisulo's nose grazed the satiny lips he found there. His long lashes closed as he inhaled her intoxicating scent. He wouldn't think of who'd been there before him but satisfied himself in the knowledge that none would come after.

Kam cried out something incoherent, she was so tortured by the delicious desire swirling throughout her body. She wanted to move away from his dangerously mesmerizing touch, but knew she couldn't. Not until she'd sampled the feel of his tongue plunging deep inside her.

At that moment, however, his nose was proving to be as pleasure providing as his tongue. It was outlining her clit and then invading the area just below it. Kam was so sensitive she could feel his breath there.

"Kami," Chisulo whispered, ragged and deep. A second later, his tongue plundered her sex. He groaned, having never experienced such gratification in providing oral pleasure to any woman. It was as though she held a hidden treasure and he'd not survive if he couldn't taste. The more he tasted however, the more he craved.

Kam's high pitched cries filled the bed chamber and she bucked her hips to capture every inch of his thrusting tongue. Chisulo rose to his knees, holding her thighs as he did so. His heavy sleek brows drew close as he dined on the swollen petals of her femininity. She was coming heavily and he was intent on drinking in every drop.

Kam could scarcely breathe; she was in such a state of sheer delight. She thrust against his mouth, the walls of her pussy clutching and releasing his tongue. An orgasmic wave flowed through her and she convulsed fiercely. Chisulo was merciless, unrelenting and tongue fucking her more vigorously. Blindly, she reached out and her nails in search of the awesome stiffness of his denim clad arousal.

A moment later, her hips bounced atop the furs. Chisulo released her as though she suddenly burned to his touch.

Leaning down, he nuzzled the softness below her ear. "Think about it," he whispered, and then left her alone on the bed and twisting in unsatisfied need.

THREE

"I won't survive it. I swear I won't survive it," Chisulo was saying later that day. His hands were braced along a stone window sill as he stood hunched and staring out at the view of the magnificent Falls. Tiring of the spectacular scene, he looked away in time to see the handsome older man across the room attempting to mask a smirk. "I'm serious Mustafa. I'd rather go into battle than be alone with her in this house."

"But she's the one you want?"

"More than you know," Chisulo practically groaned, dragging all ten fingers through his hair. "It's just these damned circumstances!" he raged.

Mustafa Nkosi stood from the corner of the desk. He crossed the study to clap a hand against Chisulo's shoulders. "You knew the rules, little brother. But look at the bright side. You're here all alone with one helluva fine piece of ass."

Chisulo rolled his eyes. "Yeah, a fine piece of ass that I can't have."

"Oh you can have her," Mustafa corrected, his own darkly handsome face softened by humor. "You can do anything you please with that beauty short of full consummation. That is, until you-"

"Tell her I killed her brother," Chisulo finished, not bothering to add the real details of Rashid Okonkwo's death.

Mustafa shrugged. "Right."

Chisulo sat on the window sill. "Tell me this Mustafa, how in the hell am I supposed to get her to come to me *willingly*- to give herself to me after I tell her some shit like that?"

"Chisulo you knew what this was when you decided that you wanted her." Mustafa reminded him. "You knew that to have Kam's heart, you'd have to rid it of whatever male held the biggest part of it. You also knew that you'd have to admit to the deed before you could truly have her body."

Chisulo massaged the heavy chords of muscle packing his forearm and watched as his brother prepared to leave.

"You also knew that Rashid's death was only a small part of this," Mustafa continued absently, checking the pockets of his loose fitting khakis for the keys to his Hum-Vee. "He would've been killed regardless of your feelings for his sister."

"But *I'm* the one who did it and I'm the one who has to make her understand *why* I did it."

"And you love her," Mustafa pointed out softly.

"I want her in my bed, that's all," Chisulo spoke in a voice that was even less convincing than the look on his face.

"You *love* her," Mustafa corrected. "You've loved her since she came into your life over two years ago."

"And if you can tell me how she's suppose to believe that after I tell her I killed her brother…I'll owe you forever," Chisulo swore, his voice holding a haunting quality.

Mustafa only grinned and leaned over to press a hard kiss to the top of Chisulo's head. "Enjoy her little brother. For the promise of soaking your dick in that, I'll bet you'll tell her before the morning. 'Night, 'night," he bid in a playful tone before leaving the study.

Chisulo sat still only a second longer, before he moved and hurtled a paper weight across the room. Fear was something he never lacked, but now it rested inside him like a fever when he was in Kam's presence. The risk of losing her-the risk of drawing her hatred was the worst of it.

For the better part of a year, he'd watched her with her brother. She loved him beyond reason and when she tended his wounds-he couldn't help but imagine her doing the same for him. She was the first and only woman he'd ever wanted to share his secrets. He wanted her beyond reason and that scared the hell out of him. Moreover, the thought of slaking his lust with anyone besides her, sickened him.

Her strength so easily matched his, her body was perfect for all the things he wanted to do with it. The way she responded to his touch…he'd be as much a slave to her as she was to him.

But she'll leave the first chance she gets and she'll want you dead when she discovers what you've done-what you are. Sadly, he had no other choice but to tell her and now was definitely not the time to lose his nerve.

***

Now's not the time to lose your nerve, girl, Kam was telling herself then as well. She remained in the room two hours after Chisulo left, before discovering that he hadn't locked the bedroom door when he'd gone. Thoughts of his sex-starved men kept her caution high, but she couldn't resist exploring the place.

Quietly, she exited the room, keeping a death-grip on her robes as she strolled the hall. A bit more confidence emerged as she neared a staircase. Quickly, she descended the stone curving well, looking back over her shoulder for any sign of Chisulo. She grew steadily confident when she didn't see him.

Where was the door? She wondered. Her brown eyes were wide with anticipation, her hair flowing wildly as she raced across the clearing at the foot of the staircase. If only she could find-

"We exit through the roof, Kami."

Kam didn't bother to turn at the sound of his voice. *Of course they did,* she acknowledged and muttered a vicious curse below her breath. Eventually, she turned to find him leaning against the doorjamb which led out to one of the long corridors.

"Besides, you'll catch your death," he warned, raking the robe that emphasized her curves. "This time of year, the Falls are as cold as they are treacherous."

Kam smoothed her hands over her arms. "I may be tempted to take my chances."

Chisulo smiled; adoring her courage as much as he did the picture she made standing before him in her bare feet. "Then at least do it on a full stomach," he suggested.

A resigned smile crossed Kam's lovely face then. "You're not gonna let me leave, are you?"

"No."

Kam nodded at his blunt reply. She let loose the breath she'd been holding and it was replaced by nerves. "You know what this is, don't you?"

Chisulo rolled up the sleeves of the mocha shirt that hung outside his jeans. "I'm not kidnapping you, if that's what you think."

Kam slapped her hands to her sides. "Then just what the hell do *you* call it?" she challenged.

"There's something I need you to know and I can't seem to find the words to tell you."

Kam went still. *The great and gorgeous Chisulo Nkosi at a loss for words?* "This must be good," she breathed, moving closer to his relaxed form. "What's this about?" she dared to ask.

"Rashid."

Kam lost her grip on the robe. The loose front fastening offered teasing glimpses of her pouting breasts- full and firm. She was so stunned by Chisulo's admission; she paid no attention to the helpless intensity on his dark face as he studied her.

"How do you know my brother?" she asked.

Dragging his midnight stare to Kam's face, he shrugged. "I know he was killed. My men watched you bury him."

Kam shook her head, a half smile tugging at her mouth. "You talk like your men are ruthless savages, yet they let me bury my brother in peace."

"Well," Chisulo smiled and shifted his weight from one sandal shod foot to the other. "They aren't *all* savages."

"How did you know his name?" she queried.

"They heard you speak it."

"How did you know he'd been-been killed?"

"Judging by the way you stormed into your house, emerged with a crossbow and set out like you were chasing the devil…I can only assume you were after the culprit." He fixed her with a probing midnight stare. "May I ask?"

Kam shuddered. "A lion-a black bastard of a lion slaughtered my brother."

Chisulo smirked at her description of her brother's killer. "Couldn't he defend himself?" he asked, purposely attempting to goad her. "Surely he didn't need his baby sister to come to his rescue."

"You jackass, you know nothing about my brother!" Kam snapped, but quickly reigned in her temper. "Rashid could never pick a fight like that. He only went out for a walk, nothing more…" she trailed away, her thoughts returning to the horrific scene she witnessed between her brother and the gigantic cat. The vengeful stirrings were reawakened and again, she fixed

Chisulo with a scathing glare. "If you aren't kidnapping me, then you have to let me go. The longer I waste time here, the further away-"

"He roams my property," Chisulo interjected, watching her eyes widen with excitement. "You're welcomed to stay if you like. Perhaps you'll…catch sight of him."

Kam padded across the cool stone floor beneath her bare feet. She was preoccupied by thoughts of revenge. The chance to get her hands on the animal now filled her with a happiness she'd not felt since before she discovered Rashid's secret. The elation swirled through her, until it could not be contained. Turning to Chisulo again, she threw herself against him and enveloped him in a tight hug.

"Thank you, thank you," she gasped, crushing herself against his massive chest.

He knew it was the anticipation of a kill that ruled her actions. That fact didn't diminish the affect they had on Chisulo. The moment her lithe, voluptuous body touched him, his shaft began to swell.

Kam realized what she was doing only seconds before his hands closed about her upper arms. In the next instant, she was backed against the doorjamb. Her moan of pleasure mingled with pain as the crude length of the jamb pressed into the small of her back. Her moans ceased when his tongue invaded her mouth and began a slow, torturous exploration. Her response was immediate, her tongue swirled over and under his while she rubbed against his powerful frame. His hands cupped her full buttocks to lift her high against the doorjamb. Kam let her tongue trace the even ridge of his dazzling teeth, and then returned to explore the recesses of his mouth.

He was twisting her this way and that and Kam was desperate to feel the massive swell of his cock against her-inside her. Tiny cries were gargled in her throat as their kiss grew more savage.

Awkwardly, she began to grind her hips against him. "Please," she found herself begging for the second time that day. Faintly, she was surprised by the depth of her desire for this man-regardless of how devastating he was. But she was sick of her need being awakened, teased yet unsatisfied.

"Please," she urged him once more and moved to insinuate her hand between them. Her actions were almost frenzied in their quest to free him from the sagging denims he sported.

A savage sound, much like a growl built inside Chisulo's chest. *Stop her*, his voice of reason insisted. He responded by gripping her ass more securely and allowed his middle finger to graze the super sensitive spot between her derriere.

Kam cried out, her lips weakening as his tongue continued to explore deep within her mouth. Chisulo's middle finger had slipped inside her hole and an explosive yearning set her aflame. She could feel the heavy streams of come easing past the dark flesh there. Desperately, her hand returned, working to undo the buttons securing his jeans. She tore her mouth from his and looked down-stunned to find that the buttons had yet to burst free of their own accord. His cock was of unbelievable proportions and Kam believed she'd be just as pleased to see if the organ looked half as good as it felt.

Again, as though he were jerking out of a trance, Chisulo released Kam. He let her slide down the jamb as he dragged a hand through his hair. Kam struggled to catch her breath and frowned when he turned his back toward her.

"I'll come for you when dinner's done," he said and left her alone.

***

Kam returned to the bedchamber as if in a daze. *I'll come for you when dinner's done,* that's what he said. Did he mean it literally? *Lord Kam, shut up! The man is playing you for a fool, can't you see that?!* She berated herself, slamming the door behind her.

Hissing a curse, she stomped into the adjoining bathroom. There she began to run water in the sunken back porcelain tub that covered much of the floor space. Her thoughts were so focused on what happened-what *almost* happened with Chisulo. So much so, that she took no heed to the fact that the cabinets were stocked with every delicious fragrance of bath and shower gel a woman could want. Absently, she added a coconut scented creation to the tub and waited for the water to rise.

Downstairs in the kitchen, Chisulo slammed pots to the stove with more force than necessary. Grimacing, he leaned against the grey marble counter top and resituated his cock for the second time that day-no good. He needed to fuck. He needed to fuck the chocolate beauty who pranced half naked around his house. The little interludes they'd shared were growing more pitiful and weighing dangerously on his temper and his restraint. If he didn't come clean with her soon, he was left with only two choices: get her the hell out of his house or take her body and risk losing his own.

"Fuck!" he raged, hurtling another pot across the brick floor.

Mustafa was right. He was in love with her. It was about more than her body; desirous as it was. He couldn't tell her the rest. He'd be free to help himself to her body, but not her heart-never her heart. Unfortunately, her heart couldn't do a damn thing for him just then. He needed to take her and then he could think. Then, he could figure out the rest.

Kam lost track of how long she spent in the tub. The scent of the foamy bubbles was intoxicating and made her want to stay there drifting in and out of consciousness forever. For almost ten minutes, her fingertips had been grazing the folds of her sex. Her pussy felt tight-ripe with desire. A desire only Chisulo Nkosi could quench. Sadly, he seemed unwilling to carry things to that level and she felt too damned relaxed to try again to figure out why.

Praying she wouldn't grow too loud once she got started, Kam let the tip of one perfectly shaped nail delve just inside her core. Tugging her bottom lip between her teeth, she grew bolder and thrust her index finger deep. A soft cry lilted in the air as a rhythm ensued. After several minutes, she craved more and added her middle finger to the thrusting and rotating caress. Soon, the bathroom was alive with a medley of feminine moans of satisfaction.

"Kami?" Chisulo called, knocking softly before he pushed open the bedroom door. His dark, deep-set gaze narrowed at the sight of the empty room. He was about to leave; figuring she was off exploring some other part of the house. Then, he heard it and instinctively, his head tilted toward the bathroom door.

His mouth curved into the beginnings of a soft smile the closer he came to the sounds. *Damn, would she sound this way when he was buried to the balls inside her?* Chisulo asked himself. His cock switched gears from semi-hard to throbbing stiff at the sound of the delightful shrieks she emitted. Unable to resist a peak, he opened the door and observed. His legs weakened at the sight of her dark body surrounded by heavy bubbles. They swished around the black tub as she writhed and bucked. Her eyes were closed, her head resting along the leather padding around the tub as she cried out.

Commanding strength to his legs, Chisulo left the bathroom. He shut the door without her ever being aware that he'd been there. He closed his eyes tight, desperate to quell his own desire. He could still hear her orgasmic shrieks however and ordered himself outside the room. In the hall, he wracked his brains for something else to focus on-anything that would clear his mind of the image of Kam in that tub pleasuring herself into a frenzy.

Once he'd recaptured some semblance of control, Chisulo went back to the bedroom door and pounded his fist to the thick pine.

"Kam?!" he called, hearing the water slosh more frantically in the tub.

"Um, yes?!" she replied in a shaky voice.

"Dinner's done. Hurry up before it gets cold."

***

"This is incredible," Kam complimented in hopes of stirring conversation. She was being truthful of course; Chisulo had rustled up a delicious feast of curried chicken, wild rice and greens with moist wheat rolls and wine. Just then, they were in the midst of dining on a delicious fruit tart he'd presented for dessert.

"So tell me about this lion," she said, venturing upon the topic she really wanted to discuss. Her heart lurched when he pinned her with his charcoal stare. She had his attention at last.

"What would you like to know?" he asked.

Kam set her coffee cup aside and leaned back in her chair. "Does he happen by every now and then or do you see him frequently?"

"I see him almost every day," Chisulo replied, sitting back as well. "Exactly what do you plan to do when you see him?"

Kam's smile was cold. "I plan to kill him."

"With what?"

"With *what*? Dammit Chisulo didn't your men bring my weapons or were they *ruined* along with my clothes?" she snapped, her expression clearly accusing.

He chuckled at her nerve. "Love, have you taken a very good look at that thing?" he mused, sloshing a bit more wine into a crystal goblet.

"I watched that *thing* attack something already wounded and weaker than it was. In my eyes, it's no bigger than a kitten."

Chisulo settled back again and regarded her with hooded eyes. "It could kill you inside of a second."

"I disagree."

He laughed aloud then and wondered how many times her admirable courage got her in over her head. "You disagree?" he probed.

Kam shrugged and toyed with the sleeves of the robe. "He looked right at me that morning and did nothing."

"So what? You think that means he'd allow you close enough to kill him?"

"It's a chance I'll take."

Chisulo felt his amusement turning quickly to agitation. "Are you done?" he asked and began to clear the table when she nodded.

"Just how do you acquire all these artifacts?" Kam was asking as they took an after dinner stroll along the corridors of the mansion.

Chisulo looked up at the towering Nubian statues that guarded the entry to one of the hallways. "I've traveled-everywhere I believe. My family is huge and we've always valued history very strongly. I guess you could say I come from a clan of collectors. My younger brother Haddad and I have sort of been entrusted to keeping the collection safe while our older brothers tend to more important issues."

Kam studied the various weaponry and stone carvings lining the corridors. "I can just imagine these pieces in that beautiful museum I designed," she teased, though her pride was evident.

Stopping mid-stride, Chisulo turned. "As beautiful as the lady who created it?" he asked, his onyx gaze appearing to smolder as he stared down at her.

Kam swallowed and put space between them, hoping to avoid another lusty encounter. "So about the lion," she sighed, "how many of your men has he slaughtered?"

Her matter of fact tone sent Chisulo's fist to clenching. "He's not a man-eater," he informed her.

"He *wasn't* perhaps," she corrected, following him inside the darkened ballroom at the end of the hall.

A definite draft chilled the room and Kam stood just inside, rubbing her hands along her arms. Chisulo left her there to go flip the switch located in the depths of the spacious room.

"Perhaps if your brother had been…himself, the lion may not have attacked."

The chill touching Kam's arms seeped through to her bones when she heard his voice in the darkness. The lights flicked on and she was staring at him on the other end of the ballroom. "What are you saying?" she breathed, stepping forward.

Chisulo folded his arms across the mocha shirt he wore. "I think you know," he said and leaned next to a towering column.

"What do *you* know?" Kam challenged.

"I know Rashid was a shifter."

Kam could only take one step forward before losing the ability to move. "How?"

"Because he and I had that in common," Chisulo confessed.

Kam looked on in stunned and horrified amazement. Before her eyes, Chisulo Nkosi shifted into a massive onyx lion.

FOUR

How could she have not suspected? Kam marveled, having fallen to her knees when Chisulo made the miraculous transformation. Aside from the fact that he now padded on all fours, the black cat and Chisulo Nkosi were unarguably similar. They were sleek, huge and magnificent to look at.

Chisulo's ebony skin, eyes and hair made him a human replica of the deadly lion. The wild dark hair, mustache and beard…God how could she have missed this?

Kam remained on her knees. The mosaic silk robe pooled about her as she turned in order to maintain eye contact while Chisulo slowly advanced. Then, he let loose a gruesome roar, which resounded like a thousand drums within the high ceiling ballroom. Kam fell back, and then quickly scurried to her feet and raced out the door.

***

She paced the bedchamber, searching her surroundings for anything else she could prop against the door. Taking a moment, she allowed herself to process what she'd just witnessed. He was a shifter! He was the lion who had killed her brother!

The chairs at the door rumbled. They jostled against each other beneath the sudden pressure behind them. Cursing her cowardice, Kam perched on the middle of the bed. She closed her eyes when the door crashed open and Chisulo entered. He'd resumed human form, but Kam didn't know if that sent her more or less on edge. He was completely, devastatingly nude. For a time, Kam cleared her mind of everything except the delicious image of him. A shudder riddled her body when her gaze dropped past his waist. Her pussy contracted at the sight of his erect and massive dick. The sensation was so overpowering, she actually moaned.

"You stay away from me! You son of a bitch, I swear I'll kill you!" she raged afterwards, desperate to maintain her anger and not be consumed by the whirlwind of lust threatening to claim her. She reached for the lamp on the bedside table and hurled it towards him. Chisulo cleared it effortlessly.

Kam shook her head. "How could you?" she whispered. Her voice carried in the stillness. The room was bathed in black except for thin streams of moonlight that flooded the hallway and doorway.

"You don't know everything. There were reasons," Chisulo said, thinking how very pathetic the words sounded in the darkness.

"Reasons?" Kam almost laughed. "What reasons bastard?"

Muscles danced wickedly along Chisulo's jaw. He knew she deserved answers, but then there was only one thing he wanted to give her. His cock was always at its heaviest and hardest just after he shifted. He'd told her the truth and she was now his for the taking. The coconut foam she'd bathed in clung to her skin and had tortured him all during dinner. Until he felt her wet pussy sheathing his dick, he wouldn't be able to focus on another damn thing.

"Chisulo?" Kam called, when the door closed and the blackness descended fully. She felt her heart lodge in her throat and she backed toward the head of the bed. The room was as silent as it was dark.

"Chisulo?" Kam whispered, not really expecting him to respond. She was inching back even closer to the towering headboard, when her ankle was imprisoned in an iron grip. She strained against it, attempting to break free but was dragged-without ceremony-to the center of the bed.

Kam kicked out blindly, touching nothing but darkness. Before she could push off her back, she was pinned down. "Damn you," she raged, bucking against Chisulo in hopes of toppling him off her.

The effort was fruitless of course, Chisulo barely budged. In the process of the tussle, Kam lost her robe. She gasped, her nipples hardening instantly when they grazed the steel wall of his chest with repeated, delicious nudges. Her lashes fluttered while she still struggled against the building mound of sensation welling within her. His mouth trailed from her neck to collarbone, before he added his tongue to the act. He was like a man possessed, licking and lathering her skin with bold, savage strokes. Kam's fist slammed his shoulder and she grunted her frustration that mingled with need.

Chisulo raised his head. "Do you really want me to stop?" he asked, praying she'd say no since he didn't know if he could.

Kam said nothing and he took that for the answer he wanted to hear. The next sound in the room was a low growl rumbling in his broad chest. The guttural sound combined with that of his lips and tongue suckling her ever hardening nipples.

"Chisulo," Kam gasped when his hands folded over her wrists and pinned them to the fur covered bed. She ached to entwine her fingers in his silky, midnight hair. His mouth feasted on her tits, outlining their shape, inhaling the scent within the valley between. He settled over her and they both shuddered at the sensational friction of their skin meeting without the hindrance of clothing.

When he released her wrists, Kam splayed her hands across his chest. Her exquisite gaze widened in the darkness when she touched the unyielding slabs of muscle. He was unreal, she thought, stroking his pects, her thumbs grazing his nipples. Unable to resist, she arched up and captured one between her lips. A triumphant surge swirled inside her when he grunted a pleasurable response. His body felt sleek, hard, void of any hair and fragrant with the scent of wood and wind.

Kam discovered that once she tasted him, she couldn't get enough.

Still tonguing and suckling his nipples, Kam eased her fingers along the chiseled length of his torso. She hesitated but a moment when she at last touched the light smattering of silky hair just above his erect dick. She bit her upper lip and prayed he wouldn't stop her.

Instead of withdrawing, Chisulo took her hand, encouraging her to complete the journey. Kam let loose a whimper when her fingertips just grazed the silken head of his cock. He sat hunched above, careful to keep his full weight off her. The position allowed her to lie back and relax as she explored the stunning length and width of his shaft. She abandoned the dark, pulsing rod momentarily to test the strength of his thighs which were massive and as rock solid as his dick. His ass was taut and round beneath her palms. Boldly, she cupped and stroked his balls, hearing the slow release of breath he expelled as a sign of his satisfaction. Once again, her hand curved around the swell of his cock. As she'd suspected, it was long and felt wondrously powerful. Chisulo jerked each time her fingers ventured further along its length.

Kam moaned as well when she attempted to close her hand around him and couldn't. Her breathing resembled tortured pants and she questioned whether she'd be able to accommodate the impressive endowment.

Chisulo's fists were pressed on either side of Kam's arms as he sat above her. His breathing grew more labored while the coconut scent rising from her skin intoxicated him as much as her touch. As aroused as he was; if she continued to work her hand along his shaft, he'd be coming all over them both. He pushed away her hand and curved both of his beneath the swell of her ass, tugging her closer.

Kam's gasp mixed with a scream when she felt the tip of his dick nudge just inside her creamy walls. Inch, by rock solid inch the organ invaded her body and Kam was sure the thing would tear her apart. Chisulo held her thighs firm, his big hands flexing each time she tensed. He kept her spread wide, unmindful of her trembles and tiny whimpers. She was too weak to do anything but take it. She felt her walls stretch anew as the throbbing organ filled her.

"Chisulo…" she sobbed, aching from the sweet sensation of pleasure on pain. It was as though she'd never been fucked before. Well…she hadn't-not like this.

He kept her thighs trapped upon the bed as he claimed her. Kam writhed in frustration, wanting to arch and rotate her hips. She cupped her breasts and began to squeeze the pouting mounds while her thumbnails grazed her dark, firm nipples. The more deeply his cock invaded her quivering core, the heavier she came. Kam's lashes fluttered when she felt the moisture streaming down her thighs. Muffled slurping sounds filled the room when he began to thrust inside her. After only four or five lunges, Kam felt ready to orgasm. Then, she realized he wasn't even fully inside her-still more inches to go.

"Chisulo, I-I can't," she groaned, twitching her thighs still trapped in his grasp. "I can't take it," Still, she bucked her hips in hopes of capturing more of his steel length.

Chisulo's rough chuckle filled the bedchamber. "Oh, I think you can," he argued and drove the rest of his dick inside her. His head ached; his mind was so full of ways he wanted to pleasure her.

Just then, he was in sheer heaven. She felt like silk drenched in heavy cream as her pussy gripped and released him. He didn't want to come-not yet. Unfortunately, a full day of foreplay had depleted his self control. Kam's helpless cries in his ears stroked his ego as thoroughly as her core gloved his cock.

Drawing one of her long, shapely legs across his shoulder, he rammed her with unrelenting strokes. Mercilessly, he took her, stretching her with every plunge. Heavy grunts rose from his throat, his eyes closed as he sought to brand her with his sex. Again, Kam splayed her fingers across his massive chest. She cried out sharply when he tongued her calf with slow steady strokes while rotating his hips, stirring his wide shaft inside her twat.

Kam's sharp cries, softened to weak sobs while Chisulo's growls of satisfaction gained volume. Her eyes widened in disbelief when she felt him stiffen even more. Moments later, a wealth of come spewed deep inside her.

***

"Why did you kill him?" Kam asked much later that night while they lounged atop the tangled covers.

She lay parallel to the headboard as he reclined diagonally across the bed-a forearm thrown across his eyes. The door was open and the room was partially lit by moonlight.

"You know what I am," he said, his tone requesting no response. "For centuries, the clans of big cats have been in a constant struggle for dominance. It's in our nature to fight," he explained, his deep voice carrying a haunting, hollow quality. "The Panther, Tiger and Lion clans…from the time I could walk, I was being schooled on the power struggle existing between us in human and feline form," he told her.

"So you just killed my brother because that's the way it's always been done?" Kam asked, pushing herself up to ask the question.

Chisulo bristled and followed suit. He planted his feet on the fur rug covering much of the stone floor. "There's more to it than that."

"More?"

"You."

"What?"

"Kam," he began, a murderous scowl further darkening his face. *Jesus, this is going to sound completely insane,* he thought. "When a member of one clan decides to take, as his high companion, a female from another clan, there's a price. Such a thing is not encouraged."

Kam laughed. "Discrimination amongst cats?" she mused.

"Exactly."

Suddenly, Kam shook her head. "My God Chisulo, do you hear yourself? This is complete nonsense."

Chisulo massaged a bicep and silently agreed with her. "It's true," he said.

"Just what the hell are you trying to tell me? Because I really don't see what any of this has to do with you murdering my brother."

"Jesus Kam, it wasn't like that." He shrugged off his approaching frustration. "To have you, I had to eliminate the male who held your heart. To have you, I had to kill Rashid."

A noxious wave rumbled in her belly. Kam seemed to convulse as it ran its course inside her. Three times, she opened her mouth, but no sound emerged. In place of sound, her rage mounted and in the next second, she was pummeling Chisulo's back with double-fisted blows.

Like before, he allowed her to vent her sorrow and fresh anger. When she finally collapsed, exhausted against his back, he turned. Cupping her neck in his hand, he held her still for a searching kiss. She couldn't help but to respond. With a whimper, she thrust and rotated her tongue around his. The groan he uttered in response plunged her back into reality. As though she were realizing who she was kissing, Kam wrenched away from him. Madly, she raced into the bathroom and started the shower.

In the bath, Kam rested her head against the shower's black tile. The deep breaths she inhaled couldn't rid her mind of the thoughts ravaging it. She'd just given herself *very enthusiastically*, to the man-the animal who massacred her brother. What sickened her most was that she'd not lost sight of that as they rolled around fucking fiercely in Chisulo's bed for the better part of three hours. Her anger-her remorse even was pushed away someplace deep the second he touched her. A million showers couldn't erase the mark he'd made on the place he'd taken possession of. Chisulo Nkosi seared his brand somewhere in her soul-a place only he could find.

In spite of the hot shower spraying against her body, Kam felt cold. Instinctively, she knew Chisulo had decided to join her. She couldn't force herself to turn and face him. Her decision suited Chisulo just fine, he moved close behind her. The water seared his chest to her back when his hand curved over her hip to pull her next to him.

"Don't," she sobbed, already nudging her bottom against his erect penis.

Chisulo was silent. His hands spanned her slender hips squeezing them before curving around to pump her full bottom in his palms. Slowly, his hands ventured upward and cupped her pouting breasts.

Kam shuddered amidst the sensation of water pelting her skin and hair combined with his thumbs grazing her nipples. She kept her hands plastered on the tile. Now, she was grinding her ass more insistently against him. Chisulo only stroked her nipples with the tips of his thumbs and smiled at her heated moans for more. When she leaned back her head, Chisulo hid his gorgeous face in her lengthy wet tresses. His hand abandoned her tits to resume the journey along her ribcage and abdomen. He massaged five fingers against the baby soft triangle of skin above her womanhood and trailed his tongue along the nape of her neck when her head sloped forward.

Kam bit her lip and flinched when his thumb began a torturous assault on her clit. The sensitive bud tensed and tingled for all his affection and he delighted in plying the nub with gentle squeezes and slow fondling. Kam was so aroused, she laughed at the pleasure of it. The sound rose above the steamy water spray, into the moonlight beaming through the high windows in the bathroom. Maintaining his sensual torture upon her clit, Chisulo let his other hand initiate a second attack on her labia. He manipulated the fleshy mound with his thumb, then smoothly inserted his index finger and thrust slowly. He grunted his own satisfaction when a load of hot cream covered his skin. Her thighs shifted suddenly and he added his middle finger to the shocking caress.

Kam satisfied herself riding his fingers and gasping her appreciation when he allowed four fingers to pleasure her at once. Still, her frustration mounted, she wanted more.

"Yes, please yes," she begged when he positioned his heavy shaft between her buttocks. Obligingly, she stood on her toes to allow him easier entrance. She ordered herself to relax, preparing for the painful intrusion. Smoothly, Chisulo began to impale her upon his engorged sex. He shuddered amidst her shrieks of satisfaction. The feel of her tight ass sheathing his cock imprisoned him inside a haven of sensation.

"Jesus Kami," he gasped, resting his forehead upon the tiles. He absorbed the feel of taking her so savagely. He held her upper thighs more firmly as he filled her with his length.

Kam was torn between grinding or riding his fingers that continued to rotate inside her sex. "Please," was all she could manage. She wanted to feel his dick inside her.

Meeting her request, Chisulo spread her buttocks just slightly-allowing his massive erection deeper penetration. He took her slowly and allowed her to receive and enjoy only a few inches of his dick before he gave her more.

"Dammit...Chisulo."

"What?" he asked, suckling her earlobe as he plundered the full tight cheeks of her ass. "Tell me," he commanded, when she only gasped in response. "Tell me," he ordered again, thrusting his middle inside her pussy, his thumb nudging her intimate flesh while burying his cock to the hilt.

"Dammit, fuck me," she commanded, moving back against him in a helpless, desperate fashion.

Chisulo's thrusts were immediate and savage. He took her without regard for the tortured cries she began to utter especially when she eagerly met his every lunge. He closed his eyes, savoring the hot water drenching his face and hair that plastered over his head and neck in glossy, onyx ringlets. His gorgeous dark face was sharp with desire and he growled his approval at the moonlit glimpses of her creamy come coating his dick each time he plunged into her perfect rear. Finally, he trapped her thighs in a vice grip and stopped her from moving at all.

Kam's molasses toned nipples grazed the tile and she loved the sensation it roused. Her mouth slackened, falling open and she groaned into the darkness when his cock thrusts grew steadily unrelenting and thoroughly rapacious.

"Damn, I don't want to come yet," he rasped, into her shoulder. Of course, he knew he'd lost all control of that decision.

Kam grunted when she felt his warm release ooze inside her. She'd come the moment his dick invaded her and several times afterward,

For a time, they stood limp against the shower tiles. Their bodies remained connected, while they enjoyed remnants of aftershock sensations.

FIVE

Kam woke the next morning-er afternoon-feeling more relaxed than she had in years. For a moment, she thought *years* may have been an exaggeration but realized it was pretty much right on the mark.

While she lay there cozy and delighted in bed, she took note of a few things. Most obvious, she found that she was nestled amidst real bed coverings of crisp champagne linens instead of luxurious furs. In fact, she was in a different bed-a different room all together. Beautiful cream fringed rugs partly covered the hardwoods of the oak paneled dwelling. Wrought iron lamps filled every corner and she could see past the double doors that led the way to the balcony. On a sunken white arm chair not too far from the king bed; with its towering oak and mahogany trimmed headboard, were a slew of undergarments.

There had to be over two dozen articles of clothing in that chair, she thought. Whatever the count, there was

enough to pique her interest and pull her out of the bed.
Her bare feet sank into the plush rug when she stepped
over to observe the pieces. Her brown eyes widened as
she took note of the fact that they were all her size-right
down to the underwear. Kam couldn't prevent a smirk.
Hell, Chisulo Nkosi should know that size better than
anyone. After all, he'd held her ass in his hands for the
better part of the night, hadn't he?

Kam shook away the images that threatened to
make her wet. She moved to the window, something
she'd sorely missed during her stay in Chisulo's pitch
black bedchamber. Her eyes widened when she
discovered the views past the window. Absently, she
took a seat on the padded sill and marveled at the view.

Victoria Falls. It was as gorgeous as she'd always
heard. The pictures she'd scoured in books or on
television couldn't come close to the true beauty in her
line of sight. God, a woman could get used to this, Kam
thought while curling up on the sill. Then again, there
was no reason for her to *get used* to anything. She had no
reason to stay, now that she knew more than she ever
wanted about the onyx lion. Lord if *that* wasn't enough to
wrap her head around…

She'd always believed Rashid had been the victim
of some horrible curse. To discover it was a common
occurrence-Chisulo made it sound like a veritable honor.
Still, the fact remained that he had killed her brother.
Faintly, she recalled him saying there was more but
dismissed the thoughts from her mind. Anyway, she
wanted him more than she'd ever wanted any man. She
had to get out of there. No need to waste more time.

Chisulo had gotten what he wanted. It wasn't a week, but he'd survive. So would she. She'd have to, before she did something really stupid and fell in love with him.

***

Kam took a shower and decided to wear one of the frocks Chisulo had provided among everything else. The one she chose was a solid cream color that emphasized the flawless beauty of her dark skin. The bodice scooped, allowing her abundant bosom to bubble at the tops while the spaghetti straps slid adoringly off her shoulders. The dress fell in luxurious folds at her feet and trailed slightly behind her in a beautiful casual fashion.

The sun streaking in when she awoke, had given way to clouds and rain by the time she ventured outside her room. So much for a tour of the Falls, she thought. Instead, she'd decided to grab a bite to eat and remain indoors for another day. She'd tour the Falls in the morning and be on her way. Out of Zimbabwe and away from Chisulo Nkosi.

Speaking of which, where was her sexy host? Venturing outside the room, Kam located the stairway and headed down. On the first floor, she peeked inside various rooms. She found him in a den. He dozed in a massive wine suede lounge chair. The huge plasma screen television was tuned to a sports channel, but the volume was barely audible. Kam realized she'd not visited this room during their tour the day before and decided to browse while Chisulo slept. She spent several moments surveying the masks and statues that lined the walls and bookshelves.

Her attention soon returned to Chisulo and she couldn't resist staring at his incredible features. Stepping closer to the lounge, she indulged herself. Lightly, her fingers grazed his beard. Her lashes fluttered while she recalled the delicious friction of the silky midnight whiskers brushing her thighs as he feasted between her legs.

"Stop Kam," she told herself and started to back away.

Chisulo caught her wrist before she could venture too far away. Kam strained against his grip when he pulled her down to him. She wasn't surprised when her efforts to resist had no affect. His dimpled grin flashed and he looked completely at ease.

"Anywhere, anytime," he recited and gave one final firm tug which landed her in his lap.

"I didn't come here for this," Kam gasped, though she gradually grew pliant when his hold on her grew less confining and more massaging.

A quick cry escaped her mouth when he released her wrists and slid his hands along her thighs pushing up the folds of the dress along the way. Kam pulled her bottom lip between her teeth, and kept her brown eyes focused on his dark ones. Chisulo's expression was devilishly intent and seductive. His fingers curled into the drenched crotch of her panties and a second later the material ripped under the pressure of his hand.

Kam felt her thighs tremble and ignored the knowing smile widening his sensual mouth. His thumb thrust past her pussy lips and into a well of fragrant moisture. Taking a fistful of her dress, he raised her off his lap and unfastened his jeans. He was swollen and painfully stiff against the zipper and grunted satisfactorily when the massive erection was released from its confines.

Effortlessly, he settled Kam back atop his lap and eased her down onto his ready shaft. She moaned in helpless fashion, her fingers curving into the soft fleece of his sweatshirt as he filled her. Her pussy walls seemed to flex and contract in unison. Chisulo directed her movements which suited Kam fine since she felt incapable of doing anything other than receiving his hungry arousal.

Chisulo's forehead was marred by a fierce frown as his big hands tightened around her bottom. He squeezed his eyes shut tight while savoring the exquisite feel of heat and come surrounding his dick. Massaging her behind, he gave the full dark mons harsh taps as they bounced against him. The telltale slurping sounds filled the room. Kam was coming uncontrollably and buried her fingers in her hair when she threw back her head.

Keeping her impaled on his penis, Chisulo sat up and let her pull the sweatshirt from his back. He responded in turn by ripping the dress from her body. He reclined against the lounge, his hands covering her glorious breasts as they jiggled before his face.

Kam took stock of his rugged Gortex boots which were planted firmly on either side of the lounge. His jeans were tugged down just enough to free his steel cock while her own body was entirely bare. She felt an electric shudder of decadence jolt through her.

Chisulo kept his hands cupped around her bosom and eased up to bury his face in the valley between. His lips and tongue instigated a sensuous assault on the milk chocolate nipples that instantly puckered and hardened. Tortured cries fluttered from her lips when his perfect teeth grazed the nub of one breast as his middle finger stroked the other. Kam shivered when his mustache and beard tickled her flawless bare skin. Her hips moved clockwise, before she moved up and down his huge shaft. Every slow bounce mounted more juice from her pussy.

Chisulo fell back against the lounge and allowed her to take the lead. He watched her work over him. Her hips rolled seductively and his deep set black stare was drawn to her toned abs and the perfect tits that pouted above. He'd wanted her from the moment they met to discuss the museum project two years prior. Thoughts of when-*if ever*-he'd have her like this ravaged his mind for nights on end.

Now, she was here. She was here and riding him like he was her favorite stallion-moaning like she'd never been so pleasured before. The reality of it, made his balls twitch and soon his release was flooding her. Kam eased her hips movements, but did not stop completely. She loved the way he jerked each time she contracted and milked his dick for the very last drop of his release.

***

Black River, Jamaica

Ali Okonkwo's handsome face was a picture of expectancy when he saw his younger brother approaching his open office door.

"Anya? Anya? Let's finish this later, alright?" Ali asked, gathering a stack of files and passing them back to his assistant. He waved his brother inside while the plump young woman hurried from the room.

"Any word?" Ali asked, once the door closed behind Anya.

Taisier Okonkwo grimaced and dragged a hand across his clean-shaved head. "No trace of them down there," he announced, massaging his eyes as he spoke.

"And your people are sure they even went there in the first place?"

Taisier sighed and pushed both hands into the deep pockets of his salt and pepper trousers. "We know they both purchased tickets to Zimbabwe. The compound at Batoka is the only place they'd go. Besides, their clothes are still there."

Ali nodded dejectedly; his dark brown face wore a weary expression. Suddenly, his temper mounted and he slammed everything off the desk. Just then, Ahmed and Kwame Okonkwo arrived.

"No word still, I take it?" Kwame noted, seeing the clutter on the floor surrounding his brother's desk. "This is getting serious," he groaned and took a seat.

"The truth now," Ahmed urged his older brothers. "What do you think's become of Kam and Rashid?"

Ali and Taisier exchanged glances.

"We should prepare ourselves for the possibility that they might be dead.

"Fuck!" Ali roared, slamming his fist upon the empty desk before he stood. "I don't want to hear talk like that Taisier," he all but growled.

"Ali," Ahmed stood, approaching his brother's desk on tentative steps. "With all respect, Taisier may be right."

"Stifle that shit, Ahmed," Kwame ordered.

Ahmed only raised his hands defensively before he massaged his neck. "Damn, is there anyway to go through this without them?" he wondered.

"We could…" Ali began, sitting on the edge of the desk. His back was turned toward his brothers. "We could do without Rashid, but having Kam is of necessity. None of this will be possible if we don't have her cooperation."

"And Saiida is certain?" Ahmed asked, referring to their cousin.

"She is," Ali confirmed, smirking a bit as he stroked his square jaw. "And since she's our lead chemist and the only ground breaking scientist I know personally, I'm apt to take her word."

Everyone in the room bristled, conceding Ali's point. The situation was setting each of them more on edge with every passing day.

"Well, what if-"

"Ahmed," Ali called, finally turning to face his brother. "There is no way around this. I've asked every question and got the answers to a few I never thought of, trust me," he stood and rolled up the sleeves of his slate green shirt. "The serum must be prepared in the precise manner in order for it to work properly. We can veer from none of the procedures."

Silence filled the office until Taisier's cell rang and he took the call. The brothers listened; taking note of

Taisier's responses which were brief and grew harsher the longer he spoke. The group was watching expectantly by the time he completed the call and took a seat on the nearest chair.

"That was Zuri Mbeze," Taisier shared, leaning forward to brace his elbows on his knees. "He's heading the search team out in Zimbabwe."

"What news?" Ali prompted.

"They found a makeshift grave about a half acre from the house. It was Rashid. Zuri told me he'd just been buried…no more than a few days," Taisier buried his face in his hands and groaned.

"What about Kam?" Ahmed asked, stepping closer to his brother.

Taisier shook his head. "No sign of her."

"What do you think it means?" Kwame asked.

Taisier looked to Ali.

"If our sister is dead, this is done." Ali pronounced.

Kwame folded his arms across the cannabis leaf emblazoned on the sweatshirt covering his broad torso. "And if she's alive?"

Ali turned his back once more. "Then our enemies have her and are wondering how best to use her. If they realize how important she is…she won't be alive for long."

***

The next morning, Kam donned a scandalously tight pair of denims with a rose petal cotton top and trekked down to the stables. She enjoyed a visit to the Falls and then went to check on her horse. Coal was healing nicely and Kam was confident he'd be ready to travel back down to the gorge any day. The news, however, was bittersweet as a curse hissed past her lips.

Hell, what woman would want to leave such an exquisite place? She reasoned. Of course, that was only a small part to her dismay. Chisulo Nkosi was a gorgeous dark male whose smoldering sex skills were the stuff orgasms were made of. Sadly, that fact didn't diminish the reality that he'd taken from her the one thing she loved most in the world. Knowing that it was a part of the scheme of things; or because he was so desperate to have her, did nothing to cushion the blow. She wanted Chisulo for as long as she could have him. Additionally, she wanted the black lion dead. Unfortunately, one could not exist without the other.

Chisulo had prepared breakfast and ventured out for Kam. He found her in the stables, but chose not to disturb her right away. Clearly, she appeared to be in deep thought-he could easily guess the topic. Easing one hand into the back pocket of his sagging light blue denims, he watched her-loving the way she moved. His dark gaze was trained on her lush bottom filling the seat of the jeans she sported. The top she wore left her midriff deliciously bare and had his fingers itching to rip it away for him to bury his face in her breasts.

Grunting softly, Chisulo looked away, knowing where his observations would lead. In moments, he would be experiencing the uncomfortable and; as of late, all too familiar tightening below his waist.

"Looks like he's almost ready to travel," he said, deciding conversation was in order.

Kam nodded, feeling his heart jump to her throat at the sound of his voice. "Yeah," she sighed, smoothing her hands across Coal's neck and back. She grimaced, as she was unable to disguise her voice with excitement.

Chisulo massaged his neck. Something ached in the pit of his stomach. He didn't want her out of his sight and felt powerless to do anything to stop it.

"Chisulo," she whispered then, resting her forehead against Coal. "Why is this...*war* necessary? *Is* it necessary?" she asked, turning to face him then.

Chisulo shrugged and rested his tall frame against the stable doorway. "There's always been some sort of struggle," he confessed, tugging the sleeves of his burgundy sweatshirt above muscular forearms. "My father fought...*his* father fought..."

"So it just goes on and on? No questions? You all just-just accept it?" Kam asked, the expression in her almond shaped stare becoming as incredulous as the tone of her voice.

Chisulo's frustration marred his magnificent features. "You think solving this thing is as easy as a handshake and an agreement to friendship? It's not," he whispered, dragging a hand through the glossy darkness of his hair.

Kam rolled her eyes and focused on the hay littering the stable floor. "It could be," she muttered.

"Hell Kami, not when your brother's are..."

Kam looked up, her eyes narrowed in suspicion. "When my brother's are what?" she probed, leaving

Coal's side to close the distance between them. "How are my brothers involved in this?"

Suddenly, the frustration left Chisulo's face and was replaced by realization. "You don't know, do you? You thought only…"

"What?" Kam almost begged, and then folded her arms across her chest and urged herself to calm. "Please don't keep this from me Chisulo.
Too much has been revealed for you to start keeping secrets now, you know that." She finished, looking up at him in challenge.

The muscle twitched along his jaw as he considered her point. "Sit down," he said at last.

"I'll stand," she decided.

He nodded, moving past her and deeper into the stable. "Rashid wasn't the only one in your family who could shift."

Kam seemed to deflate. She clasped her hands to her chest and leaned against a wall. "My brothers? They knew?"

Chisulo's dimpled smile appeared. "Oh yeah. They're no different from Rashid. Shifters from birth-just like the rest of us."

Kam shook her head which was beginning to ache with the receipt of the new knowledge. "So what? Your family wants to kill off every shifter alive in some power play or-"

"No Kami, it's not like that."

"Then what's it like?"

Chisulo stroked his beard. "It's suspected," he began, trying to choose his words carefully. "Actually, it's a fact that your brothers are on the verge of developing a serum that; if successful, will reverse the shifting phenomena permanently. If brought to creation, this serum would be a powerful tool. Not only would it reverse and prevent, it would also…induce. Whoever possesses it would possess the power to play God if they chose. They would have the power to create an army if they wished."

Kam was massaging her forehead and watching Chisulo as though he were speaking in some foreign tongue. "You're all crazy," she decided, raising her hand when he opened his mouth to respond. "And I was right. "This is all some power play," she added.

Chisulo shrugged. "Be that as it may, the serum has its benefits," he championed. His face held a stoic expression as his onyx stare traced the lofty heights of the stable. "Those who didn't want their lives ruled and affected by this affliction could be free of it-forever."

"And that's worth killing for?"

"I believe your brother thought so."

Kam stiffened at his mention of Rashid, but didn't lash out. Chisulo was right. How many mornings had Rashid awakened in pain and talking of a miracle that would rid him of the shifting he despised. She squeezed her eyes shut quickly, fearing tears were about to appear. "If this thing has such a potential for good, why can't you fools just come together and work out a compromise?"

Chisulo smiled, absorbing the soft, lost tone in her words. He thought of how perfectly her name suited her. Kamili Tamu- *sweet innocence and perfection* in Swahili.

What she'd suggested had no chance in hell, but it was the sanest opinion in centuries of unrest.

"Kam you've got no idea of what sort of life this is," he said when he realized she was still waiting for his response. "Rashid obviously kept you shielded, which is why he left you alone every evening. It's not a glamorous life," he said, walking over to stroke Coal's back. "In spite of the majesty associated with the big cats, it's a gruesome existence. You've been blessed to be spared this, when the rest of your family-" He stopped, his attention riveted on his own words.

Kam paid no attention to his silence. "My brother was killed over some miracle drug that hasn't even been invented yet," she raged softly, turning her tear-streaked face toward Chisulo. "No matter how much he dreaded his existence, I'm sure he didn't want that," she said and then turned and left the stable.

***

Versoix, Iceland

Rani Nkosi sloshed another healthy portion of strong black coffee into a massive mug before flavoring it with an equally healthy dose of Kahlua. "How valid is this source of yours, Kofi?" he asked.

Kofi Nkosi stroked his cleft chin and smiled at his older brother. "It leaves no room for doubt," he confirmed.

"I don't like it," Mbaku Nkosi spoke up from his post across the office. "I can't fathom the Okonkwo being so foolish as to set up a facility right under Chisulo's nose."

"Sometimes it's best to hide in plain sight of your enemy," Mustafa Nkosi mused.

The others nodded in agreement with their eldest brother.

"And since he's gone now…" Mbaku noted.

"With their sister," Kofi recalled.

"Do you suppose they suspect anything?" Kofi wondered, resting against the edge of Mustafa's desk. "Surely, they've gone to the compound at Batoka and seen their brother's grave," he shrugged. "It could be only a matter of time before they realize who lives above the gorge."

"They'll never find him, but that's not what worries me," Mustafa said, massaging the strong ridge of his jaw. "Our younger brother is in love with the key to the Okonkwo forming their serum."

"But Chisulo doesn't know that. Neither does the young woman," Mbaku pointed out.

Mustafa grinned. "But *we* do," he challenged. "I don't like to think about how badly this could turn out," he said, moving to take his place behind the long cherry wood desk. "If she has to be sacrificed, I wonder if he'd be as enthusiastic for the deed to be done as he was when he eliminated her brother?"

***

Kam felt relaxed and content while she enjoyed her moonlit view of the Falls. Dressed in yet another exquisite lounging gown of satin and chiffon, she savored the calming vision from her place on the red suede settee before the bedroom window. The last few days had been like a dream, a dream she was reluctant to have come to an end.

She felt completely spoiled and entranced by the beautiful mists that rose from the rushing falls as they bubbled and foamed below. She was so captivated; she almost missed the knock on the bedroom door.

"It's open," she called, waiting for Chisulo to enter.

He moved quietly and with ease walking around the back of the settee. Kam leaned back her head when his hand smoothed across her hair which was drawn back into a loose, elegant ball. Finally, he took a seat facing her on the long chair.

Kam smiled and shifted her gaze back towards the open windows. "For a year, I've dreamed of seeing the Falls and now I have my own perfect private view complete with a devilishly comfortable chair to enjoy it from."

"And a devil to go with it?" Chisulo probed, wanting a hint at her mood towards him then.

Snuggling back on the settee, Kam studied her host. "A devil comes in handy sometimes," she purred.

"Does he now?" Chisulo teased softly, though his charcoal stare harbored something more intense.

Kam tugged her bottom lip between her teeth, her eyes falling helplessly to trail the curve of his mouth. A moment later, her upper arms were imprisoned in Chisulo's iron grasp. Her heart thundered in her ears when he pulled her up snug against his broad chest. She moaned when his tongue thrust deep, filling her mouth and exploring every nook and cranny when it rotated and stroked. Instantly, she began her own exploration of his magnificent body. Torturously slow, she eased her hand along one of his massive thighs and whimpered when she came in contact with his erection stiff and pulsing beneath his jeans.

Chisulo grunted, his sleek brows drawing close as he broke the kiss. "I'm sorry that I upset you earlier," he whispered, resting his forehead against hers while he spoke.

Kam was breathless and took a moment to respond. "I want-needed to know. Did you tell me everything?" she asked.

Chisulo dropped his head to the crook of her shoulder and winced. "I've been honest with you," he said, smoothly evading a more truthful response. He couldn't figure exactly why he'd yet to tell her the truth about Rashid's death. Perhaps it was easier to have her believe the worst of him. To tell her that her brother's death was an accident-that he'd had no intention of killing him…and have her not believe him, would be a million times worse.

Kam accepted the explanation. Silently, she decided to take him at his word. After all, it couldn't have been easy to admit to killing Rashid much less being a shifter. She was still stroking his cock, loving the way it throbbed just slightly beneath her hand. The delicious sensations forced Chisulo's eyes to close while he focused on the pleasure.

"You need to eat," he said finally, his baritone voice impossibly heavier in the wake of desire. "I'll be down in the living room," he said and pushed himself up from the settee.

Kam didn't bother to change for dinner and entered the living room some ten minutes after Chisulo had left her. She'd have to leave tomorrow-she confirmed in her mind on the way down the staircase. To stay another day would seal her fate and she knew it. Chisulo Nkosi was already like a drug she needed to sample each day in order to get through the hours. Thankfully, it was only her body that was hooked, not her heart-her soul or so she'd hoped.

Yes, tomorrow she was out of there. Tonight? Well, tonight, she'd enjoy the mastery of his touch for the last time. The lower level of the mansion was almost completely black when Kam took the last step down. She made her way to the living room which was aglow from a fierce blaze that churned in the fireplace.

Chisulo had prepared yet another feast. Stewed beef in a heavy sauce of onions, scallops and herbs awaited in a deep silver tureen. Steamed brown rice, a mixture of broccoli, carrots, asparagus and snow peas with moist pumpernickel rolls rounded out the meal. For dessert there was a sinful apple crumb cake. Everything was set out upon the furry silver gray rug that rested before the stone hearth.

Chisulo was reclining on a long sofa, his arms folded across his chest. One denim clad leg hung over the side of the chair while the other rested on the overstuffed olive green cushions. His deep set midnight gaze was focused on the blaze. For a time, Kam helped herself to the beauty of his profile stern with concentration.

"Hope you're hungry," Chisulo warned, having already sensed her presence.

"Starving," she replied, hoping her husky tone of voice would give him no clues as to what she was truly *starving* for.

Without looking her way, Chisulo moved from the sofa and began to prepare her plate and then his own.

"This looks incredible-as usual," Kam complimented only to have Chisulo reply with an absent 'mmm hmm' in return. Clearly, her host wasn't in a talking mood just then.

It was just as well. The crackle and pop of the blazing logs provided the conversation as they dined. They each refilled their plates and wine glasses twice during the meal.

"More?" Chisulo inquired, watching as she set aside the remnants of her second slice of apple crumb cake.

Kam could only wave her hand in decline and watch as he cleared away the serving dishes and plates. She was curled up and content on the sofa by the time he'd finished with the kitchen duties.

"I'm leaving tomorrow," she announced, when he took his place on the end of the sofa opposite from where she sat. "I-I just need to-"

"Hold it," he whispered, raising one hand to urge her silence. "There's no need for you to explain to me."

"But there is," Kam argued, smoothing her hands across the satin sleeves of her gown as she spoke. "I want you all the time," she admitted, managing to maintain eye contact even when he turned his probing black stare on her. "It makes me sick with guilt because I should want you dead and here I am fucking my brains out with the man who killed my brother." She shook her head and smoothed back a lock that had fallen loose from her chignon. "It's too much Chisulo," she sighed and rested back upon the sofa as though she were exhausted. "And I'm too much of a coward to fight against it."

"You're no coward, Kami. Far from it," he muttered, silently acknowledging that she was the most phenomenal woman he'd ever met.

"Hmph," Kam retorted, "You'll forgive me if I don't share your sentiment," she added.

"Hey," Chisulo whispered, reaching out to pull a bit of her gown between his fingers when she moved to leave the sofa. With one tug, he made her straddle his lap.

Their throaty kiss resumed. Kam could scarcely moan amidst the ravenous lunging of tongue. Then, however, she wanted more than his tongue inside her mouth. She broke the kiss and began to lavish his neck and gorgeous face with soft lip pecks. She massaged the breadth of his chest beneath the material of the T-shirt emblazoned with the lion logo of his favored Manchester Monarchs hockey team.

With Chisulo seated on the sofa, Kam slid to her knees before him. She made quick work of his button fly, tugging her bottom lip between her teeth when what she yearned for sprang free. Her almond-shape stare followed the path of her fingers as they gripped and caressed his massive erection.

Chisulo smiled, sparking his dimples at once. He adored the awed look in her lovely eyes as she surveyed his build. She gasped and her eyes met his in delight when he flexed the stiff muscle, causing it to vibrate in her hand.

Kam leaned closer and trailed the tip of her tongue from the base to the head of his dick. She took time to lavish the satiny tip of his manhood with several eager caresses from her tongue. Then she repeated the torturous stroking, each lick growing wetter as her enthusiasm intensified. She took special care with the head of his cock. Slowly, she suckled, her tongue outlining the surface and circumference. Chisulo's responsive grunt was low and savage when she suckled more of him. His hands were clenched into fists upon the sofa cushions when she enveloped his full length in the moist warmth of her mouth. He was so impressed; he wanted to watch her perform for as long as he could stand to. He was finding more and more to love about Kam and stared intently as she suckled his erection like it was covered in chocolate with the promise of more cocoa sweetness if she sucked with enough fervor.

Again, Chisulo's head fell back to the sofa and he dragged one hand through the glossy, onyx locks of his hair. Kam tugged on his thighs to pull him farther down and he obliged her unspoken request. His hand covered the coil of hair on her head and easily unraveled it. He took a fistful of her glorious tresses and began to direct the movements of her head.

Kam moaned at the masterful gesture and braced her hands on the sofa cushions as she took more pleasure in the demanding blow job. Chisulo was thrusting into her mouth and both hands were lost in her dark hair by then. Kam was nibbling the rigid length of his dick. Her hands were weighing and gently squeezing his balls which forced a long moan from Chisulo's throat. Her head moved up and down more rapidly while she alternated between sucking his throbbing erection and tonguing the tip of the head.

Suddenly, Kam felt Chisulo trying to push her away. "What?" she queried amidst his actions.

"I need to come," he groaned.

Kam giggled as best she could, knowing why he was pushing her away. "Please do," she urged.

The permission seemed to pleasure Chisulo as much as the sight and sensation of the beautiful woman who was marathon-sucking his cock. His response was instant and abundant. Kam continued to sheath his dick in her mouth as it filled with his release. With she'd milked him dry, Chisulo pulled her off the floor and kissed her deep.

Kam favored his tongue with as much enthusiasm as she had his manhood, which was reloading for another round. She raised her hips when he began to tug at the folds of her lounging gown. She gasped, allowing his tongue deeper exploration of her mouth. The material of her gown was bunched at her waist. Her bottom was deliciously bare and stung when he smacked it in rapid succession.

Rock hard and expectant, Chisulo's erection was hungry for more. He wasted no time setting Kam down on the lengthy steel rod. The walls of her pussy contracted and molded to his dick while he cupped her ass and directed the rise and fall of her sex on his.

Thoroughly and deliciously weakened, Kam rested her forehead on Chisulo's shoulder. Happily, she allowed him to take control. She was limp with desire, but she was throbbing and wet and ached to be continuously filled by him and him alone.

"Shit," Chisulo groaned raggedly, his big hands squeezing her bottom tighter and forcing her still.

Kam convulsed, feeling him release another wealth of liquid inside her. She began to move again-just barely rotating her hips. Breathless laughter lilted from her lips when she felt the final spasms that sent him vibrating inside her.

SIX

Black River, Jamaica

The displacement Kam felt; from the time she left
Zimbabwe to the time the plane landed in Jamaica,
dissolved the moment she arrived at her villa in Black
River.

Just a short distance from Negril, Black River was
a beautiful yet peaceful oasis from the hustle of the
tourist's haven. Once the driver left her bags in the entry
way and had driven off, Kam stripped nude and left her
clothes in the foyer. She then headed out to the sunken
stone trimmed pool in the backyard. Silently, she thanked
the caretakers for their attention and maintenance of the
villa during her lengthy absence.

She crossed the short bridge that connected the
patio to the pool area. Kam's body and mind felt
exhausted as she gazed upon the still, turquoise water.
Diving in, she indulged in a few laps which helped to
clear her head and wash off the frustrations of the trip.

Kam allowed a weary smile to show. Chisulo Nkosi hadn't been a frustration, she admitted while leaving the pool. God, how she wished he had. It would've been so much easier to leave if he had. After their sex romp the night before, they adjourned to separate bedrooms. That morning, he remained conspicuously absent; giving Kam the privacy to prepare herself, grab a quick breakfast and leave the house.

Taking a bath sheet from the chrome cabinet in a far corner of the patio, Kam toweled off then sprawled nude on one of the lounges lining the white marble walkway surrounding the pool. The sun warmed her body as it simultaneously warmed her temper. Her thoughts were turning towards her brothers and she focused on her real reason for returning to Black River. It was time to confront the brood whom she now believed were as responsible for Rashid's death as the onyx lion that killed him.

***

Versoix, Iceland

Chisulo decided a confrontation with his brothers was also in order. He'd spent the majority of the morning in Zimbabwe after Kam left. He knew he'd go crazy if he spent more than a day there without her and made his plans to leave soon after she'd gone.

Suddenly, his ethereal oasis instilled nothing for him, but a miserable hollow feeling. Dammit, he'd gone and done the one thing he swore he'd never do. He'd allowed a woman access to his heart. Kamili Tamu

Okonkwo had thoroughly ruined his legendary sexual appetite for any other woman. All he wanted, all he could think of was Kam in his bed and himself between her legs.

Yes, she had his heart, but did he have hers? Fool, he hissed silently. She'd point blank told him she felt sick with guilt each time they fucked. He was no expert on matters of the heart, but that admission sounded like a far cry from love. He realized then why he really hadn't told her the entire story. He wanted her to stay with him precisely because she was in love with him. Not because her conscience was eased about his role in her brother's death. Still, a part of him wouldn't accept that her feelings weren't running along a path that was almost vaguely similar to his own.

Hell, how had this become so complicated? He raged, dragging a hand through his dark locks as the question resounded in his mind. He'd known what he was doing when he took her into his home. Disguised then as the onyx lion, he'd practically baited her deeper along the gorge. He'd purposely frightened that blasted horse into throwing her, so that both of them would require several days rest. He'd had no intentions of letting her go. Not only was she the woman he wanted, she was the Nkosi's leverage to obtaining possession of the serum formula.

The longer he spent in her presence however; *inside* her body, the fuzzier his part in the plan became. When his treacherous heart became an unexpected part of the situation, he knew he wouldn't hold her if she didn't want to be held. Besides, there was no way he could

allow her to come with him to Versoix. He had business
with his brothers. There were suspicions that required
confirmation. If they had kept anything from him, God
help them.

Shelby Lemans' blue eyes sparkled merrily when
she saw Chisulo Nkosi strolling the long corridor leading
to the president's suite. She thrust forward her already
outstanding bosom in hopes of drawing more than a
smile and polite nod from the dark, delicious Nkosi.

"Chisulo what a lovely surprise," she greeted her
accented tone of voice low and inviting.

"Shelby, always a pleasure," he replied.

Leaning forward just slightly, Shelby trailed her
fingers across the dipping neckline of her ice blue
sweater. "It could be more of a pleasure than you know,"
she said.

Grinning, Chisulo only shook his head. "My
brothers free?" he asked, maintaining his usual
gentlemanly manner for the executive assistant.

"We're always free for you Chisulo," Shelby said,
her lovely stare trailing his powerful frame.

Chisulo's grin remained in place. He was well
aware how greatly the curvaceous redhead desired to bed
each of them. He was sure one or maybe all of his
brothers had tested her delights on several occasions.
He'd actually surprised himself by not partaking of the
sexual satiation she offered. Now, of course, it was too
late. *Happily* too late-he was pleased to admit.

"Thanks Shelby," he said, leaving her with a heart
melting wink before heading down the corridor.

Shelby's gaze followed him, admiring the cut of the tailored three piece slate gray suit he wore.

Chisulo peeked into the first office of the suite his brothers kept in the unassuming dark brick building in downtown Versoix. The room appeared to be empty, but for the unmistakable deep voice that resounded in the distance. Stepping inside, he followed the sound to his oldest brother's quarters nestled in the back of the other offices.

Mustafa was in the middle of a conference call when the door opened and Chisulo stepped inside.

"Gentlemen, I'll have to get back to you," he said and disconnected without waiting for a response or even a goodbye. He uttered a soft curse as he smiled and left the desk to greet his younger brother.

"This is a surprise," he raved, his hands outstretched as he strolled forward. "What the hell are you doing here?" Mustafa asked, enfolding Chisulo in a bear hug. "Everything alright?" he asked, sensing tension when he pulled back.

Chisulo shrugged, the expression on his dark face offering no clues to his mood. "Any reason why everything shouldn't be alright?" he probed.

Mustafa's coffee brown gaze narrowed. "Something you came to say?" he questioned, easing one hand into the pockets of his cream trousers.

"Something I came to ask," Chisulo corrected, glancing around the room. "Where is everyone?"

"Around. Do you need them to be here?"

"Oh yeah," Chisulo walked away from the desk while Mustafa turned to summon the others.

It took no time at all for the rest of the Nkosi clan to congregate in the main office. Everyone greeted Chisulo, but quickly got the hint that he wasn't in the best mood. The room grew silent as they all watched Chisulo lean against a far wall.

"So how long was it going to be before you told me?" he asked, slipping both hands into his trouser pockets as he regarded his brothers coldly. "Stafa? Bach? Must've been your decisions not to clue me in?"

"And what good would that've done, Sulo?" Mbaku asked, stepping closer. "The only thing on your mind was doing what you had to in order to get her and then enjoying her. Hell, you didn't need some shit like that on your mind."

"Some shit like what?" Chisulo snapped, pushing off from the wall. "Jesus Bach, this could get her killed- or is that what you fools had in mind?"

"Sulo-"

"What? What Rahi? She's the key to this whole damn thing, isn't she?" Chisulo raged softly, massaging his neck as he surveyed his siblings more closely. "It was never all about using her to ransom the serum, was it?"

"She's the key Chisulo," Mustafa spoke up finally. "Trouble is, we don't know *how* she connects to making this formula…work," he admitted, while taking a seat on the edge of the desk.

Chisulo sighed heavily and dragged a hand through his hair. "So what? You figured on her and I losing ourselves in each other for however long it'd take for you to find out?" he asked, grimacing when he received no answer. He realized he didn't need one. Muttering a curse, he stormed out.

"Sulo!" Haddad called, prepared to go after his older brother.

"Haddad," Mustafa called, simply raising his hand to forbid it.

***

Kam focused on her plum plumps, absorbed by their melodic swing as she sat before her brothers. "Rashid and I felt completely alone over the last four years. When this happened, when his…shifting grew too uncontrolled and he came to me…I knew I had to go. I *wanted* to go," she admitted firmly, smoothing her palms across the flaring black skirt. "When he…died and I buried him, it never once crossed my mind to call any of you." Her provocative stare was cold in its intensity. "We've lived together our entire lives and calling to tell you our brother was dead never occurred to me."

"Kam-"

She raised her hand. "No Ahmed," she said, stifling whatever words of consolation he was about to utter. "You knew. You *all* knew," she accused, standing from the mocha armchair she'd occupied at the conference table. "All this time, you knew what he was-what he was going through. You knew because you were the same thing and you let your youngest brother believe he was in the world alone."

"Dammit Kam it was never like that!"

"Ahmed," Ali called in a warning tone from his place at the head of the table.

Ahmed rolled his eyes and stormed away from his sister. "Hell Ali, she thinks we're as much to blame for his death as that thing that killed him!"

Ali simply watched Kam as she stood away from the table. "I wonder what else Mr. Nkosi told our baby sister while she was in his capture," he mused.

Kam's cocoa stare narrowed and she closed a bit of the distance between herself and the table. "Don't you give a damn about what else *he* told me. I want answers from *you* muthafucka."

"Kam!"

"Kiss my ass, Taisier!"

"Kam you're crossin' the line now."

"And fuck you, Kwame!" she commanded, before turning back to her oldest brother. "Answer me, Ali."

Ali was the epitome of calm as he relaxed in the gargantuan armchair and closely observed his sister. He nodded after a while, seeming to realize that her strength and power was genuine. He'd suspected she'd always possessed it, but had no real reason to use it. "Is it safe to assume that he told you about the serum?" he inquired, watching her nod. "Did he tell you that you're the key to its creation?"

Kam's stern expression softened with the confusion that crept over it. "The key?" she asked, reclaiming her place at the table.

The brothers exchanged glances in response to her reaction.

"Kam you're the only one," Ali informed her softly. "In the history of the three clans, you're the only one to be unaffected by the shifting phenomena. That fact alone makes you unique as well as valuable," he added. "Because you were unaffected and no one from any of the other clans even knew you existed, no one saw reason to tell you anything-especially Rashid."

"You lie," Kam hissed, her temper rising again.

"Oh he knew, Kam," Ahmed assured her. "Rashid wasn't alone. He knew what we were."

Kam shook her head once. "What are you saying?"

"When Chisulo Nkosi came here and hired you to design that museum, we knew," Ali said. "We knew they'd found out about you. It was then that Rashid decided to use your love for him-your concern to get you to go away under the pretext of helping him."

"And it wasn't easy," Taisier interjected. "You were determined to finish that project."

Kam closed her eyes. "Rashid," she whispered.

"Tell her the rest, Ali," Taisier advised.

Kam looked up, her eyes wide with expectant suspicion.

"Rashid truly hated shifting," Ali began, his closed expression finally showing signs of regret. "The stress of it began to weigh heavily on him and he was starting to lose his ability to control when he changed. News of the serum-its possibilities...thrilled him." Ali looked right into his sister's expressive gaze. "Your blood is the key, but you have to know what you're doing and why when you give it to us."

More confusion set in and Kam began to shake her head again. "I don't-"

"Unless given freely," Taisier explained, "there would be terrible consequences. Rashid was to take you away for a few weeks, inform you of the situation, give you time to process it."

"He hoped you'd cooperate once you knew everything," Ahmed added.

Ali nodded. "You were gone for weeks and then *weeks* turned into months, months…to a year and Rashid-"

"Rashid was in hell," Kam told her brothers. "The days were like one long bad dream." She held her head in her hands. "I was so afraid he was losing his mind."

"Kam," Ahmed whispered, sitting close and taking her hand in his. "This could be a miracle for so many. The chance to stop this, the madness that affects some…"

"But every wonder drug has its side effects. Does this?" Kam queried.

Ali nodded, knowing they'd revealed too much to hide any more of the truth. "There is the risk of death-we don't know the percentage. If the serum is produced, we have to prepare ourselves for that possibility."

Silence reigned for a long while. After everything that Chisulo had told her, Kam didn't think she could be any more stunned. She was wrong.

"Let's give our sister some time to think," Ali said, waving his hand as he stood. "We've told you everything," he promised when she looked at him. "We hope it's enough to help you make up your mind."

Kam was about to nod when Taisier took the seat Ahmed had just vacated. "We need you to stay close, Beauty," he urged, smothering her hand in both of his. "We don't want you to leave Black River. You can stay with one of us."

"No," Kam refused flatly.

"This isn't up for bargaining," Ahmed called.

"I'm not leaving my home."

"Kam-"

"Ali please," she urged, turning to fix on her brother who was preparing to leave the office.

"If you stay there, guards will be posted at every entrance," he warned and then turned as she was about to argue. "You don't like it, then get packed and decide which one of us you're moving in with."

The double office doors closed behind Ali and Kam realized the discussion was over.

***

Kam tossed about in bed for practically half an hour before getting up to indulge in a tall goblet of wine. She was confident the fragrant red brew would lull her right to sleep. Unfortunately, she felt even more awake when she returned to bed. Absently, she watched the gauzy white canopy curtains that billowed about the majestic wrought iron queen bed. Desperately, she focused on the mesmerizing movements of the material while it swayed amidst the ocean breeze drifting in through the windows.

Barely five minutes had passed, before Kam lost interest in yet another failed sleep inducer. Groaning, she tugged on the hem of the T-shirt she'd worn to bed and wriggled out of the top. Snuggling deeper into the crisp tousled coverings, she began to toy with her nipples which firmed quickly from her attentions. Tugging her bottom lip between her teeth, Kam allowed her nails to trail her stomach then further down between her thighs.

Parting them, she toyed with her clit, gasping sharply when sensation began to mount. Her hips undulated and arched when her middle finger thrust long and quick, amassing a load of cream. Her mind betrayed her then as thoughts of Chisulo surfaced. She imagined him there, his dick replacing her fingers and thrusting deep to increase her pleasure. Moaning her regret, Kam squeezed her eyes shut tight against the moonlight and tried to erase the image from her mind.

Refocusing on satisfying her need, Kam began to drive her fingers faster. Suddenly, a frown marred her brow, her eyes snapping open when her hand was stilled. Lifting her head from the pillow, Kam found herself staring into Chisulo's pitch black gaze.

"Chisulo? What?-"

"Shh," he urged, bringing her hand to his mouth and kissing her palm. "Do you mind if I take over?"

Dazed, Kam blinked and shook her head. The next instant, her hips rose from the bed. Chisulo had lowered his head and plunged his tongue into her drenched pussy. Kam weakened, unable to move as the delicious strokes from his tongue enveloped her in a whirlwind of pleasure. His hands folded over her hips. Trapping her upon the bed while his huge frame kept her thighs spread wide.

He feasted like a starving man, nibbling the puckered lips of her twat before rotating his tongue just inside. Finally, he plundered the farthest recesses of her sex, feeling her inner walls tighten and release. Kam's entire body arched like a bow and she buried all ten fingers in her thick locks. Eagerly, she thrust against

Chisulo's mouth, riding his persuasive tongue with all the enthusiasm she possessed. Chisulo lavished wet kisses to the insides of her thighs before kissing his way up her body.

Kam's laughter filtered the room when his tongue rotated inside her bellybutton. Quickly, he rose above her and covered her mouth with his hand.

"Quiet," he ordered softly, his baritone voice tinged with playfulness, "we don't want your guards in here now do we?"

Kam pulled his hand away. "Afraid?" she teased.

Chisulo resituated himself between her legs. "Terrified," he teased back.

"Mmm," Kam moaned, when his tongue invaded her mouth. Eagerly, she suckled every drop of her come from the lunging organ. She could feel his magnificent, granite length against her and wriggled her hips to encourage his entrance.

But Chisulo had other plans. In the midst of their kiss, he flipped Kam to her stomach. He began to kiss her shoulders with the same intensity he'd applied to her mouth. The tip of his tongue followed the dip of her spine and disappeared into the crack of her ass. Kam hid her face in the pillows and attempted to muffle her cries. She felt Chisulo's massive hands squeezing and cupping her buttocks before he spread the firm cheeks and tongued the highly sensitive area between. To torture her further, he intermittently plied the same treatment to her pussy from behind.

Kam was overwhelmed with sensation and already on the brink of orgasm. Chisulo slid his hand across her hip. His thumb stroked the satiny smooth triangle at the junction of her thighs before he moved on to fondle the achy lips of her sex.

"Chisulo," Kam moaned, desperate to keep silent but just as desperate to cry her satisfaction into the air. She arched her behind, taking in more of his tongue while his fingers explored the deep caverns of her body. She wanted to turn and face him, but he wouldn't let her. She was torn between backing up her derriere and grinding on his fingers. A powerful climax was approaching and Kam felt as if she'd burst into a million shards of sensation when his dick replaced his tongue and fucked her from behind.

His fingers continued to pleasure her pussy from the front and Kam pressed her face deeper into the pillows. After several minutes of the devastating dual fuck, Chisulo pulled Kam up and kept her secure on his cock. His big hands molded to her bouncing tits and manipulated the nipples into pleasure induced buds of desire. Kam let her head fall back and couldn't resist letting her pleasure be heard. She could feel a chuckle rumble deep through his chest before he gave her breast a warning squeeze and again clamped a hand across her mouth.

"Quiet," he ordered, driving his dick more forcefully inside her ass as if to punish her.

The action felt far from punishment for Kam. She slid up and down Chisulo's steel cock and moaned as her lips and tongue feasted on his middle finger. He was still half dressed and a delicious friction mingled from the harsh feel of his denims rubbing her bare skin.

Chisulo's rumbling groans filled Kam's ears as completely as her bosom filled his wide palms. Her nipples tingled, aching for more than the torturous thumb strokes he applied before squeezing the perfect mounds of flesh. Kam bit her lip when his embrace tightened on her hips and he forced her to still as he spewed inside her. He continued to nibble the satin chocolate skin between her shoulder blades and they remained in the embrace minutes after release.

Kam was finally so at peace, she was on the verge of losing conscience then and there. Chisulo gave her a shake and kissed her neck to rouse her.

"I want you out of here by sunset tomorrow," he whispered against her ear.

"Mmm...what?" Kam murmured, still very much out of it, her thoughts wholly focused on sleep.

Chisulo squeezed her upper arm. "Out of here by sunset," he repeated, giving her a tiny shake for emphasis.

"Out of here?" she parroted, slowly growing more lucid as she turned to face him. She covered herself with the top sheet. Blinking, she tried not to moan at the sight of him while he fixed himself and zipped his jeans.

"You can't stay in Black River, love," he told her, coolly. "You can't stay in Jamaica at all for that matter. It's too dangerous."

"Why?" Kam breathed.

Chisulo tilted his head. "Have you talked to your brothers?"

Kam's eyes narrowed. "What do you know about that?"

"I know you're the key to this serum working," he responded without hesitation. "My brothers know as well. What we *don't* know is how."

"And you're here to find out."

"I'm *here* to get you out of here."

"For my own good?" Kam asked her doubt evident.

Finally, Chisulo lost his temper and stormed to the bed. "Dammit, if I wanted to take you Kami, you'd be gone. No matter how many pathetic guards you think you've got here to protect you."

"Understood," Kam conceded with a slow now. "But I'll tell you like I told my brothers, I'm not leaving. I have a life, career, friends here…I won't leave that Chisel," she informed him, her vibrant brown gaze focused and firm. "Rashid was everything to me, but he's gone now and it's time I live my life for *me*. Black River is where I'd like to do that."

Chisulo pulled an olive green fleece sweatshirt over his head and decided to stop trying to convince her. Clearly, she wasn't of a mind to listen. He'd have to try a different tactic. If that didn't work, then the lovely Ms. Kamili Tamu Okonkwo would find herself in his capture once again.

***

The following afternoon, Kam had been invited to attend a beach party at the villa of one of her neighbors. The gathering started about two hours before sunset. By the time Kam arrived, it was in full swing. After her lengthy absence from the community, everyone wanted a moment to speak with her. Julien Dwele was particularly interested in a moment of her time. The developer had wanted Kam's input on a new industrial park since before she began the museum project for Nkosi.

"Kamili I simply want to know if you're open to me now that Chisulo is done with you?"

Rich, full laughter erupting, Kam shook her head at Julien's opening question. "Right to the point I see," she teased, folding her arms across the key hole cut in the bodice of the midnight blue frock she wore. "You do have a love of suggestive dialogue, as I've said before."

Julien shrugged, leaning close to the round intimate bar table they shared. "Well, *this* bit of dialogue is straight-forward. I want you to design this park. I haven't found anyone I want on this project as much as you and your firm. I'd like for you to come in tomorrow for breakfast and discuss it in further detail."

Kam smiled, unable to mask her delight. A new job was exactly what she needed to take her mind off...everything.

"Well?" Julien prompted, grinning widely.

Laughing again, Kam shook his extended hand.

Later, Kam ventured out towards the beach. Guests were already gathering to enjoy the sunset and she took her place among them. The majestic Victoria Falls were beautiful beyond reason, but Kam admitted she could never have her fill of the calming effect of a late evening Jamaican sky.

She stood captivated by the sun and foaming ocean waves for several moments, when a pair of arms slipped about her waist. Whirling around, she smiled at the sight of an old friend.

"I was wondering if you were here!" Kam cried, hugging Dr. Maxwell Davis.

Max grinned, squeezing Kam tight. "When they told me you might make an appearance, I knew I'd have to be here."

"Well, I'm glad my presence was enough to draw you out of that clinic of yours," Kam teased, referring to the marine studies clinic Max headed.

The handsome scientist only grinned more broadly. "I figured since you weren't the property of Chisulo Nkosi any longer perhaps the rest of us poor fools could have a chance."

Kam smiled. "I was never Chisulo Nkosi's property," she shared, her voice sweet yet firm.

Max simply shrugged. "That's what *you* thought," he argued, drawing her close before she could dispute him. "Prove it then," he challenged.

Kam shook her head. "How?" she sighed finally.

"Have dinner or a late lunch with me tomorrow?" Max proposed.

Kam fidgeted with the end of the heavy braid that coiled around her head before dangling against her shoulder. "Sounds nice…should I meet you there?"

Max appeared stunned and elated then that she'd even accepted. "I'll pick you up from your villa."

"Well now that that's settled," Kam sighed again, squeezing Max's forearm before turning her back on him, "can we *please* enjoy this sunset?" she begged, laughing when Max pulled her back against his chest.

Later Kam and Max continued to enjoy one another's company. They caught up on the last year and Max expressed his sorrow over Rashid's death. They took refuge on the dance area along the beach and swayed to the smooth jazz from the band that performed on the villa's patio. Kam let her forehead rest on Max's shoulder and savored the happy contentment coursing through her. How long had it been since she'd felt so at ease? She asked herself. She wouldn't allow memories of her time at the Falls to creep into her thoughts.

Just then, Max stopped moving. It took Kam several seconds before she realized they were standing still.

"What is it?" she murmured, her head still resting on Max's shoulder. When he offered no reply, she looked up.

Max was staring at something above her head. He pulled his hands from Kam's waist as though she was slowly but surely burning to his touch. Kam turned and found Chisulo standing right behind her. She was too surprised to say a thing, but Max was ready with greetings.

"Got a full house tonight I see," he noted. "Good to see you Chisulo. It's been a long time," his voice carried a noticeable nervousness.

Kam felt Max's hand at the small of her back. He was nudging her towards Chisulo as though the man had caught him playing with a toy he had no rights to.

Chisulo accepted the offering, his hands rising to cup Kam's hips as he pulled her snug against his chest. In spite of her desire to laugh over Max's actions, she couldn't ignore the tightening of her nipples when her breasts crushed into Chisulo's body.

"Don't be a stranger while you're on the island," Max urged, preparing to head off.

"I'll see you for lunch tomorrow, then. Around two?" Kam reminded him, her eyes narrowing when Max offered a wavering smile and limp wave. Clearly their lunch was the *last* thing he wanted to discuss.

"Looks like I ruined your date," Chisulo mused, his deep dark eyes sparking with humor as he observed Max's hasty retreat.

"What the hell are you doing here?" Kam whispered, hoping to maintain a modicum of discretion in the presence of the other dancing couples.

"I was invited," he informed Kam, easing one hand down to cup her bottom. He pulled her so close; she had no choice but to link her arms around his wide shoulders.

"So are you here to try and change my mind again?" She asked, swallowing when his fingers began to stroke the curve of her bosom visible past the scoop hole in the bodice of her glove-tight dress.

"Change your mind?" Chisulo queried absently, more absorbed in the way her breasts bubbled into the opening of the frock she wore.

Kam rolled her eyes. "Maybe I should've said 'keep tabs on who I see outside of our...relationship?'"

Chisulo frowned; she had his full attention at last. "What does that mean?"

"Please," Kam hissed, her hands curling into fists against his shoulders. "We've only been fucking each other Chisulo. It's not like we're in love or even monogamous for that matter," she pointed out, praying he couldn't hear the unease in her voice.

Chisulo brought his head close to hers. "Is that why you're making plans to go out with that fool?" he asked, shifting his gaze towards the direction Max Davis had taken.

Kam almost burst into laughter. "It's only lunch. Does that upset you? And if so, why?" she demanded to know, realizing that she was almost desperate to hear Chisulo tell her he loved her. The acknowledgement made her blood run cold.

Those words unfortunately were far from Chisulo's lips. Furious over her nonchalant attitude regarding her safety, he took her arm and led her off the dance floor.

Kam gasped, but knew any attempt to tug free of his grasp would be useless. Her heart raced when he pushed her into a secluded portion off from the farthest end of the patio.

"Are you *trying* to get yourself killed?" he raged, crowding Kam against the brick wall behind her back.

Speechless, she could only stare at him.

"I want you out of here and I'll do anything to make that happen. *Anything* Kam, do you understand me?"

Kam decided she had no desire to discover what *anything* entailed. Patiently, she waited for him to step back before she rushed past him. Non-stop, she ran from the party and took the short distance along the beach to her villa.

SEVEN

Saiida Okonkwo wrapped her arms about her slender form and focused an unseeing stare past the windows of her sitting room. She tried to maintain her stoic demeanor, but failed when the tie around her crimson robe was pulled loose. She couldn't stop the shudder from racing her spine, as a pair of palms eased beneath the silk material.

"I've told you everything," her voice grated when those hands were cupping her bosom.

Mbaku Nkosi lowered his handsome caramel-toned face into her neck. "I doubt that love," he murmured into her softly scented skin. "If I had more time, I'm willing to bet I could get the formula out of you," he boasted softly. One hand ventured past Saiida's waist, two of his fingers invading the sensitive lips below.

"Stop!" she whispered on a gasp, yet tugged on her bottom lip and lightly ground herself on the easy thrusts of his fingers.

"You know I'd stay even if there weren't more you could tell me."

Saiida rolled her eyes. "Fuck you, Bach," she moaned, doing that very thing to his fingers. By now, there were three buried deep inside her pussy. "Don't pretend that what we do is part of something meaningful," she managed, resting her head back against his chest. "You only *want* me because I've discovered the serum and I know what it takes to make it work. I've betrayed my family and given you the key to the formula. That only leaves the formula itself and you will never get that Bach Nkosi. No matter how exquisitely you fuck me," she vowed, her words ending on a sob.

Bach closed his eyes, burying his face into Saiida's bouncy crop of hair. He was thankful he stood behind her then for many reasons. Most especially, because the position allowed him to hide his disgust from her. It was a disgust he felt towards himself. Saiida Okonkwo was an elegant beauty with a complex and creative mind to match. He wanted her as he'd never wanted another woman.

Unfortunately, the serum stood between them. In spite of it all, the survival and success of his family depended on the Nkosi's acquiring it. Bach realized Saiida was trembling in his arms and he buried his face deeper into her luxurious dark brown tresses.

"Please go Bach, please…" she begged, while sliding up and down the length of his fingers. Clearly she was in no frame of mind to pull herself away.

Accepting that the feat would be left to him, Bach did as she asked. "Thank you love," he whispered, then kissed her cheek and walked away.

Saiida allowed her tears to fall freely when the front door closed behind him.

***

"Another cup of coffee, Kamili?"

"Thanks, but no. Two's my limit."

"Perhaps another slice of banana cake?"

"Julien stop."

Julien Dwele stilled and fixed Kam with his most bewildered expression. "Something the matter?" He asked.

Folding her arms across the bodice of the mocha wrap dress she wore, Kam fixed the man with a knowing glare. "Why don't *you* tell *me* if something's the matter?"

Julien set down the porcelain coffee pot and smiled. "I don't understand."

"Really?" she probed, the arched line of her brow raising another notch. "Well, let's see. We've sat in practical silence for the last thirty minutes enjoying a fantastic breakfast. Several times, I've tried to engage you in discussion about the project you were so eager to discuss last night, but it's clear you're not interested in the subject."

Julien shook his head, still feigning confusion. "Kam really, I thought you'd enjoy a nice break-"

"Stop," she ordered softly, leaning close to the table. "You're making a fool of yourself. I already know something's wrong."

Pursing his lips, Julien's posture lost a bit of its pride. "I can't give you the project love."

"And why not?" Kam managed to question softly, though her temper was already raging.

"Kam-"

"Perhaps I should've asked *who* changed your mind between last night and this morning."

Julien's laughter shrieked nervousness. "Kam, in business things like this happen. It's nothing personal."

"I see," she whispered, standing from the table. Casually, she took the coffee pot off its tray and moved to Julien's side of the table. Bending, she whispered near his ear. "Either confirm what I already suspect or suffer a dreadful accident."

"Chisulo Nkosi is a partner," Julien wasted no time sharing. He expelled a relieved sign when she set down the pot. "He's a silent partner, but that doesn't diminish the power he has. He told me last night at the party that you couldn't have that job."

Kam snatched her purse from the edge of the table. "Son of a bitch," she hissed and stormed off the patio.

***

Mustafa Nkosi remained silent while listening to his brother's debate. Mbaku had returned with information they sorely needed. The news, however, was bittersweet.

"Obviously, we'll have to take her without Chisulo knowing," Rahi noted.

Kofi nodded. "True, but that won't be easy."

"Not only will we draw the Okonkwo's wrath, but our brother's as well." Mbaku warned.

Haddad shook his head. "I don't know who I fear the most," he admitted.

"Where is Miss Okonkwo now?" Mustafa asked.

"Black River Jamaica," Mbaku clarified. "I've got a car on her." He added.

"Well then, I suggest we not waste another moment," Mustafa decided, standing and watching his brothers follow suit.

"She won't come willingly. Snatching her won't be an easy task," Rahi cautioned.

Mustafa's expression was resolved. "Then I suppose it's a good thing we need her blood shed."

***

"You son of a fucking bitch."

Chisulo's back was turned, yet he smiled easily recognizing the angry feminine voice. He'd been expecting Kam to burst into his office at any moment. He knew of her breakfast meeting with Julien Dwele and figured her to be out for blood-his own.

Of course Chisulo had asked Julien not to say anything regarding his part in sabotaging Kam's assignment to the project. Still, he knew she'd find out. Julien was no match for her should she decide to press the issue and Chisulo knew she would.

"It's alright Jade, everything's fine," he assured his harried assistant who stood next to his desk and stared wide-eyed at Kam. "We'll take care of this later," he said, relieving Jade of the folders that shook in her trembling hands.

Jade made a quick dash for the office door, scarcely looking at the tall, exquisite woman who was practically snarling at her boss. The door closed firmly behind her.

"So did you just come to curse me out Kam, or do you care for an explanation?" Chisulo asked, once they were alone.

"Bastard. I already know the explanation," Kam hissed, crossing the office suite on slow steps.

Chisulo smiled, loving the way the black leather pumps accentuated the shape of her lengthy legs.

"I wouldn't go like a good girl when you told me to, so you figured on just pulling rank and ruining my job."

His dimpled smile deepening, Chisulo took a seat on a corner of his desk. "Something like that," he admitted softly, tugging off the coat of his charcoal gray suit.

"So tell me Chisel, do you plan on sabotaging all of my work?" she asked, crossing her arms over the front of her dress.

Chisulo only shrugged. "If that's what it takes to keep you out of harm's way-yes."

"Son of a bitch."

"You called me that already."

Raising her chin, Kam closed the distance remaining between them. "Cocksucking asshole. How's that, Chisulo?"

"That one I take offense to," he said, fighting the urge to laugh.

Kam was offended as well. So much, in fact, that she balled her fists and set out to strike him. Her attempt was foiled. "I was so right about you!" she hissed, as he pulled her arms behind her back. "You could never separate sex and business."

"Not when it comes to you," he admitted, jerking her closer. "And since you're the only one I want sex from, if your business threatens that, I have to do something to change that, don't I?"

"Sick," Kam spat and wrenched herself out of his loose grasp. Smoothing back a wavy tendril that had fallen from her braided coiffure, she turned to leave.

Something in her demeanor, released the last of the flimsy restraints Chisulo had on his temper. She was halfway to the door, when he caught her. This time, the hold he applied to her arm would not be broken.

"Chisulo you-"

"Shut up," he practically snarled, his sinful dark features tight with anger. "Do you know how sick I am of this?"

Kam tried to drag her feet, suddenly unnerved by his mood. Chisulo barely noticed her straining against him as he led her back to his desk.

"I'm done fighting everyone-including you-to keep you safe," he was saying. "I'll do whatever it takes to get you out of Black River even if it means running you out of business to do it," he warned, tugging her closer.

She used all her strength then to wrench free of his hold.

Nothing worked. Chisulo's grasp was like a vice as he kept one hand clasped over both her wrists. They stood before the desk, where he used his free arm to swipe everything from the surface.

Kam's anger cleared momentarily as she realized his intentions. Her anger returned when she felt the excitement trigger the tell-tale tingling which tensed the walls of her sex. Desperate to ignore it, she resumed her struggle to free herself of his hold.

Chisulo hoisted her atop his spotless desk. Keeping one hand across her wrists, he used the other to hike the hem of her chic attire above her thighs.

"Jackass," Kam seethed, trying to keep her knees together and failing when he insinuated a hand between and easily parted them. "Freakish devil, you make me want to vomit!" she swore, torn between hate and desire. She wouldn't acknowledge the helplessness she felt when he thrust his fingers inside the crotch of her panties and tested her wetness.

"Yeah, I can tell you're completely against this," he challenged, thrusting his middle finger deep and rotating it inside her moist pussy.

Kam's lashes fluttered and she masked a groan of pleasure with a cry of disgust. "Stop," she moaned. "Mmm," she whimpered and ground a bit on his fingers as they took her with slow, possessive lunges. "Snake," she hissed again as white cream oozed past his plundering fingers. "Devil," she branded him once more while he lowered her to his desk and followed her down. "Damn you for this," she sobbed, arching her neck when his persuasive mouth trailed its smooth column. In truth, she had no idea who she cursed more-Chisulo or herself.

Once again, she had to face the facts-he held all the cards. Never had she allowed any one-any *man* for that matter such control. Not even her brothers. Of course, Chisulo Nkosi did have an edge-she'd never wanted any man as she wanted him. Moreover, she had never loved any man as she loved him.

She winced, hearing the tear of material as he ripped her panties from her hips. Kam watched; her heart thundering beneath her breast, as he freed his magnificent endowment from the confines of his trousers. Kam closed her eyes and would have turned away, but Chisulo caught her chin.

He made her look at him. "Do you want me to stop?" he asked.

Kam's eyes widened, her disappointment flashing over just the thought of it. Chisulo's smoldering dark stare narrowed further when he witnessed her reaction. The dimpled grin flashed and he began to lavish her jaw and neck with wet slow kisses.

"I didn't think so," he muttered, bathing her collarbone with his tongue.

Kam was moaning desperately and curving her pliant form into his rigid body. Chisulo suckled her earlobe, his hands cupping her butt and positioning her pussy to accept his devastating shaft. The familiar growling filled the air when he filled her. Kam threw back her head and planted her hands palm-down on the desk. Her hips rose and rotated as she moved to accommodate every hard inch of his dick. She could feel his throbbing length vibrating inside her. The pulsing sensation forced a new wave of come from deep inside her pussy. With wild abandon, she bucked her hips and slid along his hungry cock.

Chisulo cupped her ass more firmly as his strokes became merciless-more savage. He was determined to bury himself deep inside her until she agreed to anything he wanted. Unrealistic? Yes, but damn it'd be satisfying as hell to try.

Kam's cries resembled breathless pleas for fulfillment. Chisulo let his head fall to her shoulder when he felt her walls contract around his shaft. Her slow milking of his dick made him come fast and hard. They remained locked together on the desk for several moments before he withdrew.

Kam kept her eyes lowered while she tugged her dress into place. She inched away from Chisulo, leaving the desk and disappearing into the private washroom. Once done, she left the office without as much as a glance in his direction.

Chisulo stood with his back to the door, his fists braced on his desk. "To hell with this," he muttered, hearing the door close behind her. Grabbing his keys, he prepared to go after her. He was about to shrug into his suit coat, when the chimes signaling his cellular filled the air. He decided to ignore the call, but glanced at the faceplate anyway. Seeing Haddad's name brought a curious frown to his brow.

"Shit," he whispered, unable to ignore the call from his younger brother. "What?" he growled into the receiver.

"Sulo! Damn, I'm glad you answered."

"What?" Chisulo inquired again, his voice softer in light of his brother's tone.

"You need to find Kam."

"What for?" Chisulo asked, taking a seat on the edge of his desk. His brows were drawn close in suspicion.

"We know how she ties to the serum. They're coming after her. Her blood is the key to making it work."

Chisulo didn't need to be told who *they* were.

"You have to get her out of Black River. They know she's there. Bach has someone tailing her."

"Jesus," Chisulo whispered, leaving his spot on the desk.

"Hurry man," Haddad warned. "They're prepared to take her by force and in light of things, spilling her blood won't much matter to them."

***

Saiida closed her eyes, savoring the relief that rushed through her when she made it to her office unseen. She let the door close behind her and prayed there would be no crisis demanding her attention and sending some panicky assistant to her door. She was determined to stay below the radar until she could figure out a way to finish the serum before her betrayal came to the surface.

Instead of flipping the main light switch, she decided to work by a desk lamp. Setting aside her purse and briefcase, she kicked off her cream pumps and sat behind her desk. The instant she flipped on the small, black lamp, the huge imposing figure of her eldest cousin came into view.

"Ali!" she gasped, closing her eyes as she trembled. "You frightened me," she added.

Ali offered no apologies, remaining silent for a while as he studied her.

Saiida began to fidget with the gold bracelet peaking out from beneath the cuff of the chic gray dress she wore. "Is there some-something the matter?" she queried, taking note of his guarded expression.

"I didn't want to upset the others with my suspicions," he told her simply. "Not that they'd believe me anyway. Hell, *I* don't want to believe it."

Saiida blinked and shook her head. "I don't... exactly what is it that you...suspect?"

Ali stroked his jaw and focused his probing gaze at the far wall. "I'm very overprotective, you've always known that," he said, glancing toward her. "That's especially true as far as the women in my life are concerned. That doesn't just go for my sister, but for you as well."

Saiida was grateful for the dull lighting, praying Ali couldn't see how truly unnerved she was.

"At first, I was having you followed simply for your protection," he confessed and stood from the chair he'd occupied. "With Kam gone God knows where, I couldn't risk losing you too. Then, when my men informed me of your...lunch dates and overnight hotel stays with one of the Nkosi, my following you was about more than protection."

Saiida's gaze faltered at last. Her breathing came in labored pants.

"I'd like for you to tell me what you've been doing," Ali whispered, bracing his fists atop her desk. "As if I need to ask," he muttered harshly turning away when he saw her eyes pool with tears.

"I never meant for it to-to go this far Ali, you have to believe that." She swore, slapping away the tears as though she were surprised by their appearance. "I didn't even know who Mbaku Nkosi was when I met him."

"And just where did you meet him?" Ali inquired softly, his back still towards Saiida.

She shook her head, grimacing at the seemingly innocent encounter that was anything but. "A research conference. A fucking research conference of all places," she shared, brushing her fingers across her furrowed brow. "He told me he was there to give a speech. Something about how Nkosi utilized certain scientific advances in their work."

"And before the end of the convention, he was in your bed," Ali guessed in an amused tone.

"It wasn't like that!" Saiida snapped.

"I see," Ali turned a look of phony sympathy on his handsome face. "You felt that the two of you...had something?"

"Screw you, Ali," Saiida breathed, her almond gaze narrowing murderously. "You're so set against companionship-not to mention love. I could never get you to understand, so I won't try."

"I appreciate that," Ali countered, though something flickered in his gaze when he heard his cousin's assessment.

"Besides," Saiida groaned, smoothing her hands across her face. "I hadn't even created the notes on the formula. How would he-"

"Dammit Saiida, everyone knows of the prophesy."

"*Prophesy?*" she challenged, watching him with an incredulous stare. "Ali listen to yourself. Do you know how you sound?"

"This isn't about me," he reminded her and leaned over the desk again. "I want you to tell me what you told Bach Nkosi. What information did you give him to take back to that savage lot he calls a family?"

Saiida shuddered at the quiet anger filtering her cousin's voice. "Ali, I swear-"

"Answer me!"

"I only told him that Kam's blood was the key to making the serum work," she blurted, rising from her chair when Ali cursed and turned away. "Ali please I-"

"Just how long did it take for you to tell him? Did you just outright betray your family?"

"No!"

"Or did Nkosi get it out of you while he fucked you?"

Saiida was shaking and doing a poor job of keeping her tears at bay. Ali rolled his eyes, his disgust was evident.

"Ali please, please I never meant-"

"Don't," he ordered with a raised hand.

"Ali please I'm sorry, I'm so sorry, you have to know that," she swore, then boldly closed a bit of the distance between them. "Ali truly, all they know is that they need her blood. They don't know how it has to be taken."

"Save it, cousin," Ali advised, coming closer and brushing away her tears with the pad of his thumb. "If your betrayal results in my sister's death, I swear you will need all your apologies and explanations to talk us out of killing you."

***

"I was certain you would cancel our date after your hasty exit from the party," Kam teased, accepting a glass of white wine from Max Davis later that afternoon.

Max shrugged. "Chisulo Nkosi is enough to make any man step back. The last thing you want is to be caught with anything or *anyone-*" he tilted his wine glass towards her- "who belongs to him."

Kam grimaced. "For the *second* time, I don't belong to Chisulo Nkosi," she said, wondering who she was trying to convince-Max or herself.

Max only smiled clearly unconvinced. "You were the only reason he showed up at that party-the only one he wanted. I'll be damned if I was going to stand in the way of that."

Kam leaned close to the table. "Doesn't it bother you to be so afraid of another man?"

"If he were but *only* a man, I suppose it would. He's far more and I believe you know very well what I mean."

For a time, the only sound was the soft jazz wafting through speakers and the soft clapping of Kam's sandals as she clicked the sole against her heel. Shaking her head, she set aside her glass and folded her arms across the ruffled bodice of the coral off shoulder dress she wore.

"Let's forget about last night, shall we?" she urged, tossing a lock of her wavy tresses across her shoulder. "You've more than made up for it. I can't believe you had an entire restaurant booked just for us," she noted, her eyes sparkling at the sight of the posh beachfront establishment bare and elegant.

"My pleasure," Max drawled, though he appeared a bit on edge when he glimpsed his watch. "Speaking of which, I should go check with the maitre'd and make sure everything's still on schedule."

Kam was about to remind him that that's what the waiter was for, but she never had the chance. Max had already bolted from the table. Alone, Kam thought over all that had taken place in the few days she'd been back in Black River. Her thoughts lay especially on the serum she was supposed to be the key to-A product with such potential to be a miracle cure. There were so many in desperate need of such a creation-as she'd come to discover. Unfortunately, the same wonder drug held just as much potential for evil. If only she could be certain of her brother's intentions as far as the serum was concerned. The tiny buzzing of her cell interrupted her thinking and she was stunned to find her brother's name on the faceplate.

"Ali?" she greeted.

"Kam where are you?"

She leaned back in the chair she occupied. "Having lunch with a friend."

"Where? We'll send a car for you."

"We're not done yet."

"Yes you are, love."

"Ali-"

"Dammit Kam, argue with me once you get out of there."

The urgency in Ali's voice was about as confusing as it was unusual. "What's going on?" she inquired slowly.

"The Nkosi know everything love and they know where you are. You failed to shake them when you were ditching the guards *I* put on you."

"Ali," Kam sighed, rolling her eyes. "I'll be leaving shortly and I'm perfectly safe here," she said, just as the sound of something smashing rose in the distance.

"Kam? Kam?" Ali called, having heard her gasp.

"Ali, I have to go," Kam said quickly, shutting off her cell before her brother could utter another word. "Max?" she called, spotting a figure whisk by somewhere across the dim depths of the room. "Max?" she called again, not really expecting an answer. Slowly, she stood, grasping a steak knife that lay next to her plate.

She'd taken no more than five steps across the dining room when they swarmed. In seconds, she was surrounded by at least seven men. She brandished the knife, her fierce courage dwindling as she studied her adversaries. Boldly, she advanced; knowing the way out resided past them.

The group moved forward. Their hands raised in unison to ensure an easy capture. Kam focused on an open space between two of her would be captors. She moved quickly, but not quick enough to escape the man who closed on her from behind. Still, she struggled; using the wedge heels of her sandals to inflict enough discomfort to make him release her. She clipped his shin and his hold weakened as he grunted in surprise. Using the opportunity, Kam rammed her elbow into his gut and then turned the tables-grabbing his forearm and shoving him into his accomplices. She turned and raced out of the restaurant, stumbling only once as she came out of her shoes.

Confident that she was home free, she risked a glance behind her. Stunned entrancement filled her maple brown gaze when she saw that her pursuers were shifting into lions.

EIGHT

Kam ran all the way to her villa; which thankfully, was located just a short stretch from the restaurant on the beach. She didn't stop to panic, but went straight for her weaponry. She barely had time to ready her bow and arrows before the beasts were at the door. Their heavy bodies pummeled the wood and Kam watched in horrified fascination as it splintered and cracked.

Drawing on her confidence, Kam reminded herself that she was at her best with a crossbow. She spread her bare feet and aimed the weapon at the door. Her skill was in top form that afternoon. She managed to wound several of the pouncing cats. With an agility of her own, she fired accurately from various spots in the living room and stairway that lead to the second level of the villa.

She was making her way toward the top of the stairs. Her plan was to barricade herself in her bedroom, climb down the trees next to the balcony and then make for the garage where her Jag was stored. Her foot had just touched the landing, when she backed against something-*someone* tall and unyielding. She saw the arms encircling her body and knew at once who it was. She acknowledged then that any thoughts of escape were folly.

"Let me go," she ordered anyway, still struggling against him. "Damn your soul to hell Chisulo Nkosi! I was a stone fool to have ever trusted you!"

"And exactly when was that Kam?" Chisulo growled against her ear when his mouth pressed next to it. "Exactly when did you ever trust me?" he went on.

Kam had no use for further talk. Desperate to free herself, she continued to kick wildly-hoping to strike his legs or something more vital. A pained gasp hissed past her lips, when Chisulo flexed his arms about her slender frame. He turned her to face him then forcing himself to ignore the fear in her lovely eyes.

"Forgive me, love," he whispered, before rendering a blow to her cheek that knocked her unconscious. Kam slumped against his chest and he lifted her close. Gently, he brushed his fingers across her cheek and nodded slowly when he was satisfied there would be no bruising. The last thing he wanted was to hurt her any more than he had already.

"Fuck," he grunted, frustration over the present circumstances filling him with an ever increasing rage. Gingerly, he eased Kam across his shoulder, and then signaled to his men that it was time to go.

***

"You believe her?"

"I do."

The Nkosi brothers knew better than to question Mbaku any further. The man's relationship with the lovely scientist Saiida Okonkwo had always been off limits to discussion. This time was certainly no different.

"Did she tell you anything more?" Mustafa asked.

Bach shook his head. "She didn't tell me about the serum, only that everything involving it was under lock and key."

"And I'm figuring she didn't tell you where?" Kofi mused.

Mbaku smiled and again shook his head. "'Fraid not," he confirmed.

"So what now?" Kofi asked.

"We need to get the girl and we need the formula," Mustafa affirmed.

"I say we go after *her* first," Kofi suggested with a shrug. "One out of two ain't bad."

"There may be a way to improve those stats."

Everyone turned to Rahi; who'd been virtually silent since the conversation began.

"She's at Black River," he reminded his brothers. "I'm willing to bet the serum formula, notes, everything is being kept at Okonkwo headquarters and the headquarters is based in Black River."

The brainstorming session was interrupted a short while later when one of Kofi's men walked into the office with news of the scene at the restaurant.

"They checked out Miss Okonkwo's villa- she's gone." Kai Obu told his employers.

"Chisulo," Rahi guessed.

"Thanks Kai," Mbaku said, waiting for the young man to leave the room. "Anyone up for a show down with our own brother?" he asked.

"This is a matter of high importance, Bach and if it means a show down with our own blood, so be it." Mustafa decided.

***

Kam winced and worked her jaw, groaning at the stiffness she felt there. She made a move to massage the sore area, but realized that her hands were bound to the bed she lay upon. Her legs were free, but tangled in the covers of the gorgeous black silk linens and comforter. Slowing her breathing, Kam forced herself to calm and took the time to inspect her surroundings. She was in a beautiful room-a magical place lit by the late afternoon glow of the sun.

Her ease vanished, the instant she spotted Chisulo relaxing in a chair across the room. A slow humorless laugh tumbled past her lips.

"Déjà vu," she purred, her almond shaped gaze narrowed and steady. "Except for being tied down to a bed, that is. Unless, you've got plans, Chisulo?" she inquired, her heart lurching when he smoothed the back of his hand across the black whiskers covering his cheek.

"I wanted you to listen to me, I didn't think you'd stay long once you regained consciousness," he admitted with a lazy shrug.

"And how did I *lose* consciousness in the first place?"

"You don't recall?"

"Cut me loose then, so I can reciprocate."

"Not until you hear me out."

"Son of a bitch, I don't want to hear anything from you," Kam spat, tugging her hands in a futile attempt to free herself. "I already know the Nkosi are aware of the part I play in this mess. I also know they sent you to do the deed of bringing me in and why shouldn't they ask you to handle it? You were so very successful at it before."

"So you figure you know it all, hmm?" Chisulo asked, moving to stand.

Kam's heart lurched yet she ordered her calm to remain in place. "I'm pretty sure I'm someplace where escaping is out of the question, so why am I tied down? One last screw before you turn me over to your brothers?"

"Do you love me, Kami?"

Such a question was the very last thing she ever expected him to ask. "I-what?" she stammered.

"Do you love me?"

"Damn you," she rolled her eyes and tugged at her bound hands once more. "You have me tied down to a bed and you dare ask-"

"Answer me," Chisulo ordered, his deep, raspy voice as entrancing as the manner in which his onyx gaze traveled her body. "Do you really believe my intention is to give you to my family? That what we do in bed is nothing more than screwing? Do you?" he prompted, adding touch to his questioning when he stood next to the bed.

Kam gasped, feeling strong fingers tracing her calf. She was naked beneath the covers and silently prayed that her body would not betray her. It was useless, of course when she was already on fire for him.

"Do you believe my feelings for you are shallow?" he inquired, dropping to his knees. His fingers were between her thighs. He leaned close, letting his mouth trail her tender jaw and along the column of her neck. "Having you in my bed is an added treat, having you in my life...that's the true pay off."

"Chisulo..." Kam couldn't continue, her thighs were already parting-desperate for his touch. She cried out, her hands straining within their bonds, when his middle finger stroked the folds of her sex. He thrust past the soft petals and into a creamy pool of desire. She arched, aching for every second of the delicious fingering. She bit her bottom lip when he stopped.

"Untie me, please," she asked, when he joined her in the bed. "Please," she whispered, watching him move down the length of her body. Her next plea was silenced once he bowed his head and plunged his tongue deep inside her. "Chisulo...mmm..." she whispered, grinding herself against his mouth.

He grunted, just as stimulated by her response. He circled his tongue inside her sex feeling her inner walls clutch and release. Her taste and her scent made his entire body tighten with the need for conquest. Squeezing her bottom, he deepened the oral fuck and drank in the resulting spray of moisture like a thirsting man.

"Chisulo please," Kam urged again desperate to have her hands free. He refused to oblige, simply withdrawing his tongue to trail it across her clit, then torturing her by nibbling the super sensitive bud of sensation. Her cries were loud and wanton especially when his fingers parted her labia and he filled her again with his tongue. "Damn you Chisulo," she sobbed, her hands growing limp against the headboard. She surrendered and accepted her captive state.

Soft growling rose from within his chest and Chisulo felt his shaft grow stiffer. He was moments away from coming and treated himself to only a few more lengthy strokes of his tongue inside her body before he withdrew.

"Mmm…" Kam shuddered. Chisulo had buried his dark gorgeous face between her tits and took several deep breaths. Then his nose began to outline their perfect shape. After a second or two, his tongue swirled one nipple and a helpless whimper escaped his throat when he began to suck and nibble upon the bud. Kam bucked herself against his powerful frame desperate for more than he was giving her.

Chisulo rubbed his thumb across the entrance between her buttocks. His mouth trailed her throat and he smirked when she flinched at the feel of his whiskers scraping her skin. Their lips met and Kam participated with an eager wantonness. Eagerly, she suckled his tongue while rubbing her pussy against the crotch of his trousers.

"Please untie me, please. I only want to touch you," she swore, kissing his jaw and neck, nibbling his earlobe when he finally fulfilled her request.

Unbound, Kam was a more willing participant. She buried her fingers in his black luxurious crop of hair before stripping him of the gray shirt that hung outside his pants. Splaying her fingers across his broad chest, she tongued his nipples and pushed him to his back allowing her lips and tongue free reign over his chiseled pects and abs.

"Mmm…" she moaned, having unfastened his pants and tugged them past his hips along with his boxers.

"Kam," Chisulo muttered, insinuating his fingers in her thick tresses. When her lips trailed the stunning length of his shaft, he tugged gently on her locks.

Kam graced him with a thorough oral kiss. Her mouth sheathed his dick with slow, wet caresses that kept Chisulo's dark eyes trained on her full lips sliding up and down his shaft. Her soft moans of enjoyment made his cock harden more each second. Her tongue swirled around the erection filling her mouth and the suckling she applied forced loud tell-tale sounds to fill the room.

"Damn…" Chisulo grunted. "I need to come," he told her.

"Do it then," she ordered, still sucking his dick fervently.

Chisulo turned the tables, curling his hands beneath her arms and pulling her above him. Kam felt her legs turn to water when she was impaled on his shaft. Her entire body quivered relentlessly, but Chisulo was merciless. He kept his hands tight on her hips, directing her up and down. Kam needed no instruction, her hips rotated and bounced until he changed the pace once more and pulled her beneath him.

One leg across his shoulder, Chisulo took her fast and hard. His magnificent features were sharp with desire as he focused his gaze on the lovely dark beauty writhing on his bed. "Do you love me?" he asked again.

"Yes," she gasped.

"Say it."

"I love you."

The words seemed to drain Chisulo of what remained of his restraint. He shivered, rapture spewing warm and deep. He collapsed atop her and Kam welcomed the heaviness, though it seriously labored her breathing.

After a while, he shifted his weight and searched her brown eyes with his black ones. "Now will you listen to what I have to tell you?" he asked.

***

"She's gone and her villa is a mess," Ahmed announced when he and Taisier rushed into Ali's office.

"The Nkosi. Those devils," Kwame growled.

"At least they don't have the serum formula too," Taisier commented, though it was clear he took little solace in the fact.

"Too bad they don't know Kam has to give her blood *willingly*," Ali remarked, his voice sounding more foreboding than usual. "The bastards may simply slaughter her to get it."

"Damn it, if only we could be sure she's on the island!" Ahmed raged.

"Chances are slim on that," Kwame offered.

Ali was on the phone. "Chisulo Nkosi has a compound in Negril. I think it's time we pay a visit."

***

Kam awakened in the throes of a delicious orgasm. She snuggled deeper into the massive bed and Chisulo gripped her hips more tightly to still her. His tongue drove inside her with relentless plunges. Kam thrust back, riding his tongue with wild enthusiasm.

Chisulo's earlier confession of what really happened the day Rashid died, had Kam reeling. She experienced renewed pain for her brother-his tortured mind and body. Where Chisulo was concerned, her love for him had merged with increased respect. He'd understood her brother's pain. Rashid hadn't been alone after all. Chisulo's love for *her* however, stayed his hand-forcing him to deny Rashid's pleas for death. That is, until fate intervened. Now, she acknowledged Chisulo's capture had come full circle. He'd assumed complete control over her body. Her heart and soul could never belong to another.

"No..." she moaned when a heavy knock was applied to the bolted bedroom door.

Chisulo seemed set on ignoring it. A low growl rose in his chest as he nuzzled his face deeper between her thighs.

"Shit," he hissed when the insistent knock rapped the door again. "Later!" he ordered, before returning to his pleasure providing chore.

"Sulo, it's urgent!" A man's voice called through the door.

"Don't stop-you're too good at this," Kam begged, urging him back beneath the covers when he moved to leave the bed.

"Let me handle this love," he asked, plying her with a kiss that grew lusty and wet as Kam thirstily drank her moisture from his tongue. "Only a minute," he promised while pulling away and fixing her with an adorably apologetic smile.

"This better be good," he snapped, jerking into a pair of sleep pants before whipping open the door. "What, dammit?" he greeted Obu Kente.

"Sorry Chisulo, but you need to come downstairs. Now." Obu emphasized, glancing briefly past Chisulo's shoulder. "We've got company."

"The Okonkwo?" Chisulo inquired, he'd hoped it'd take them a while longer to show up.

Obu was shaking his head. "Not the Okonkwo, your brothers," he clarified.

"Play time is over Sulo," Rahi announced, having been first to spot his younger brother descending the mahogany staircase.

Though Chisulo's face was void of expression, his black stare was penetrating. The glare left no question about his mood.

"We want her, Sulo. Time is an issue now," Kofi said.

"Do I have a choice?" Chisulo challenged.

Mbaku moved forward slightly. "You can choose to give her to us or we can take her from you."

"Take her from me?" Clear doubt softened Chisulo's face with humor. "That would be something to see."

"Hell Sulo, we know she's a goddess, but haven't you fucked her enough?!" Kofi spat.

The muscle danced fiercely beneath the whiskers covering Chisulo's jaw. A low sound rumbled in his throat as he fists clenched.

Kofi simply grinned. "Obviously not."

"Enough!" Mustafa snapped, knowing Chisulo was seconds away from attack. "No more games brother," he said. "We want her and if we have to go through you to achieve that-so be it."

Chisulo nodded, a half smile curving his sensuous lips. "So be it," he confirmed and the low rumbling in his chest became a full blown growl.

Of course, the remaining Nkosi came prepared for battle. In spite of their attempts to reason with Chisulo, they knew he would never surrender Kam. They couldn't blame him. Unfortunately, she was the key to a creation they were desperate to possess.

Every man, including Chisulo's own trusted group, began to shift. Seconds later, the massive room teemed with powerful raging lions and Chisulo's crew of charcoal gray panthers. Grizzly fangs and claws were shown, attack was at hand. Unexpectedly, the heavy oak front doors burst open. The lions and panthers hunched in unison, they were poised to attack.

The Okonkwo had arrived and were only momentarily taken aback by the scene that awaited them. They wasted not a moment longer and shifted. At last the scene was set, the characters in place. The three clans of lion, panther and tiger were ready.

The thunderous sounds outside the door roused Kam from bed. Frowning, she pushed herself up to sit and focused in on the noise. It was easy to distinguish the monstrous growls that filled the air. Without further hesitation, she left the bed intent on dressing. Of course, her clothes were strewn across the room. She slipped back into the coral frock she'd worn earlier. Heading towards the door, she tilted her head in hopes of determining exactly where the cats were battling.

Satisfied that she could take a peek, she twisted the knob; uttering a grateful prayer that Chisulo had not locked it. The ruckus quickly rose to a deafening pitch; the ferocious roaring seemed amplified and more terrifying. Kam took hold of her fear, cursing the fact that she was without crossbow, machete, pocket knife…anything. Spying a tall bronzed candlestick, she grabbed it from a short porcelain table and set out to investigate.

Big cats were everywhere-fighting to the death across the lower level and stairway. This was a battle Kam had no desire to be a part of-let alone witness. Searching for her best escape route, she spied a back staircase leading away from much of the melee. She was on her way down the back corridor, constantly glancing across her shoulder, when a bloodied brown lion landed before her-cornering her. His fang teeth were gnarled with entrails and he seemed prepared to add more to his diet.

Kam backed away, stumbling in her haste to escape the predator. The lion looked ready to pounce when an onyx cat of equal size rammed him into a side wall. Kam watched the scene for a split second then scrambled to her feet and raced into a den she found at the end of the hall. Heading straight for the windows, she worked frantically to undo the locks securing one.

A roar stopped her and she whirled around with a scream ripping from her throat. In seconds, the only sound in the room was Kam's breath which came in rapid gasping pants. Her eyes widened when the cat appeared to distort, its body lengthening, withdrawing in some places, shifting. Kam knew she was moments away from fainting in relief when Chisulo emerged before her eyes. She watched him snatch a pair of black lounge pants from a drawer on one of the end tables in the room.

"Come with me," his voice rasped once he'd pulled the drawstring on the pants and sealed the distance between them.

Kam backed away. "You're a dead man if I do," she predicted, shaking her head slowly.

Chisulo's dark deep stare narrowed. "I promise you I can take care of myself," he teased.

"I'm serious!" Kam cried her fists clenched. "My brothers want you and your brothers dead. You and your brothers want mine dead!"

"And what do *you* want?!" Chisulo countered, his bellow far outweighing hers.

Kam seemed to wilt. "You. I want you," she whispered, her lovely brown eyes sparkling with unshed tears. "But I want you alive," she clarified.

Chisulo extended his hand. "Come with me, then. I love you," he swore. "I'll kill anyone who tries to take you from me. Come with me," he ordered, this time not waiting for her response. In one lithe move, he drew her close, holding her high against his chest.

Kam was too exhausted to argue further. Closing her eyes, she let her head rest against his shoulder. Chisulo took her from the house to the boat that was sheltered in a cove and floating amidst the rising winds.

Once on board, Kam forced herself to look back at the villa. She moaned, sickened by the horrific fight scene that had spilled onto the beach.

"They're my brothers," she said, staring off into the distance in wonder as she watched the battling tigers.

Chisulo drew her back against him. "They're my brothers too," he noted, his voice hollow with remorse.

Kam turned, burying her face in his chest. "This isn't over, is it?" she asked.

"Not in the least," Chisulo confirmed, curving his big hands about her face. "Can you handle it?"

Kam searched the bottomless depths of his midnight stare. "If you're with me," she said.

"You couldn't pay me to be anywhere else," he vowed, then lowered his head and began to ply her temple, mouth and neck with petal-soft kisses. Lifting her again, he nodded to his captain who waited across the deck. "Get us the hell out of here," he ordered.

Unnoticed by the three clans of cats, the boat was soon pulling out of the cove and heading towards the open sea.

Erotica titles by T. Onyx are created by contemporary and historical romance author AlTonya Washington. Best known for her Ramsey series, AlTonya's love of the Erotica genre has prompted the release of two titles: *Truth In Sensuality* and the latest *Ruler of Perfection.* Look for the first full-length T. Onyx Erotica title in 2010 and the sequel to *Ruler of Perfection* in 2011.

Enjoy…

For more on AlTonya visit her website:
www.lovealtonya.com